P9-BZH-568

RAIN IS NOT MY INDIAN NAME

RAIN IS NOT MY INDIAN NAME

CYNTHIA LEITICH SMITH

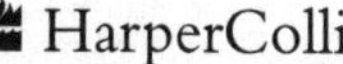

HarperCollinsPublishers

Rain Is Not My Indian Name

 Printed in the United States of America. For information address HarperCollins Children's Books, a division of HarperCollins Publishers, 195 Broadway, New York, NY 10007.

www.harperchildrens.com

Library of Congress Cataloging-in-Publication Data

Smith, Cynthia Leitich.

Rain is not my Indian name / Cynthia Leitich Smith.

p. cm.

Summary: Tired of staying in seclusion since the death of her best friend, a fourteen-year-old Native American girl takes on a photographic assignment with her local newspaper to cover events at the Native American summer youth camp.

ISBN 0-688-17397-7 — ISBN 0-06-029504-X (lib. bdg.)

[1. Death—Fiction. 2. Grief—Fiction. 3. Photography—Fiction. 4. Indians of North America—Fiction.] I. Title.

PZ7.S64465 Rai 2001 00-059705

[Fic]—dc21 CIP

AC

Typography by Karin Paprocki

18 19 CG/LSCH 20 19

❖

First Edition

For my cousin,
filmmaker Elizabeth Cole

With appreciation to: Kathi Appelt; Ann Arnold; Haemi Balgassi; Franny Billingsley; Mr. Bolton (ninth grade); BookPeople of Austin, Texas; Toni Buzzeo; Gilbert Cavazos of Mission Funeral Home of Austin, Texas; Nora Cleland; Stacy and Todd Cohen; Penny and Ron Cooper; Carolyn Crimi; Betty X. Davis; Meredith Davis; Tiffany Durham; Tom Eblen; Gail Giles; Staci Gray; Peni R. Griffin; James Hendricks; Esther Hershenhorn; Jennifer Hibbs; Frances Hill; Tracy Kasson; Jane Kurtz; Debbie Leland; Daveen Litwin; Gail McCauley; Michelle McLean; the Mid-Continent Public Library of Grandview, Missouri; Marisa Miller; Linda Mount; Nicole Onsi; Mr. Pennington (twelfth grade); the Pod; Mr. Rideout (sixth grade); Polly Robertus; Harlan Roedel; Sara Schachner; Bud and Caroline Smith; Dorothy P. Smith; Heather S. Vance; Mary Wallace; Jerry Wermund; Melba and Herb Wilhelm; Mrs. Woodside (first grade); Kathryn Zbryk; the Texas children's literature community; Toad Hall Children's Bookstore of Austin, Texas; my gray tabby cats, Mercury Boo and Sebastian Doe; and especially Anne Bustard, for pep talks and playing midwife; my very cute husband, Greg; and my personal spice girls . . . Ginger Knowlton, agent extraordinaire, and Rosemary Brosnan, editor-mentor-friend-confidante-blessing.

Tasty Freckles

FROM MY JOURNAL:

On New Year's Eve, I stood waiting my turn in the express aisle of Hein's Grocery Barn, flipping through the December issue of Teen Lifestyles*—a perfume-soaked ad for makeup, clothes, and bulimia.*

The magazine reported: "76% of 14-year-old girls who responded to our Heating Up Your Holidays survey indicated that they had French-kissed a boy."

The next day was my fourteenth birthday, and I'd never kissed a boy—domestic-style or French. Right then, looking at that magazine, I decided to get myself a teen life.

Tradition was on my side. Among excuses for kisses, midnight on New Year's Eve outweighs mistletoe all Christmas season long. Kissing Galen would mark my new year, my birthday, my new beginning.

Or I'd chicken out and drown in a pit of humiliation, insecurity, and despair. Cassidy Rain Berghoff, Rest in Peace.

DECEMBER 31

That night, Galen and I jogged under the ice-trimmed branches of oaks and sugar maples, never guessing that somebody was watching us through ruffled country curtains and hooded miniblinds. We should've known.

Small-town people make the best spies.

As we tore through the parking lot behind Tricia's Barbecue House, my camera thudded against my hip and I breathed in the chill, the mist, and the spicy smell of smoking beef. Galen's cold hand yanked mine past Phillips 66 Car Wash, Sonic Drive-In, and up the tallest hill in town to N. R. Burnham Elementary. Chewie, my black Lab, led us to the playground, and Galen grinned at me like we were getting away with something.

I thought we were.

Of course Grampa Berghoff hadn't given us permission to prowl like night creatures on New Year's Eve. Earlier that evening, he'd shelled out twenty-five bucks for pizza delivery and movies, handed me the video rental card, and said, "Watch yourself."

But Galen drew his line at chick flicks, and I drew mine at Anime. Since Mercury Videos carried only about forty titles, we'd already seen everything else.

Galen and I had gone out after the third phone call from his mother: the first to ask if he'd gotten to my house okay, a whopping five blocks; the second to ask if my big brother, Fynn, could drive Galen home—no problem; and finally to ask if Grampa and Fynn would be back from their dates before midnight. As if.

My high-tops smacked the playground asphalt, and I opened my mouth to catch a snowflake or two. Galen let go of my hand, and I dropped into the swing beside him.

We soared.

Below, Christmas lights outlined rooftops, shop windows, and the clock tower on the Historical Society

Museum of Hannesburg, Kansas. Cottony smoke puffed out of chimneys and blurred into clouds. Plastic reindeer hauled Santa's sleigh on top of the new McDonald's.

Perfect, I thought.

Besides haunting the streets and swinging to the heavens, I planned to try out the filters Grampa had tucked into my Christmas stocking the week before. I hoped to compose some shots of my hometown in all of its hazy holiday glitter.

But that's not what I was nervous about.

Glancing at Galen, I could still see my field trip buddy, the one who'd tugged me away from Mrs. Bigler's second-grade class to find turquoise cotton candy at the American Royal Rodeo. I wasn't a hard sell. With my parents' pocket camera ready, I'd hoped to shoot whatever wasn't on the guided tour. When we finally got caught, Mrs. Bigler sentenced us both to keep our noses to the brick wall for a month of recesses.

Through lemonade stands, arcade games, spelling bees, and science fairs, we'd been best friends ever since.

When Galen's rock busted out the new streetlight, we both got a tour of the city lockup. When Galen climbed the water tower and couldn't get back down, I'm the one who called the volunteer fire department.

But at Mom's funeral, he was the one who answered for me when people said they were sorry and what a shame. "Thank you for coming," he told them, just like a grown-up. And he'd asked Gramma Scott to check on me after I'd gone into the funeral home ladies' room and decided never to come out.

Galen was the one person who always understood me, the one person I always understood.

Over the past couple of years, though, something had happened. Something unexpected. Something that made me feel squishy inside. Galen's bangs had draped to the nub of his nose. His sweeping golden eyelashes made my stubby dark ones look like bug legs. He'd grown so delicious, I longed to bite the freckles off of his pink cheeks.

As Chewie barked at us from the playground below, I shivered on my swing and scolded myself for leaving the house in only my ladybug-patch jeans and the black silk blouse Aunt Louise had sent me for Christmas. But the silk made me feel sexy, more sophisticated somehow, and I'd worn it, figuring I could use all the attitude I could get.

My watch read twelve minutes until midnight. "Almost time," I announced.

"Hey, birthday girl," Galen called, "guess what I got you."

"I told you ten times that I give up," I answered, pumping my legs, trying to outswing him. "Besides, I'll find out tomorrow."

Galen and I had both been holiday babies with birthdays outside of the school calendar, and so sometimes people forgot about celebrating us. That's why he'd promised to always remember my birthday, New Year's Day, and I'd promised to always remember his, the Fourth of July. We'd spit-shook on it.

Galen's taste in presents, though, was adventurous. Over the past few years, he'd given me a frog skeleton, a bag of rock-hard gum balls, and a midnight blue Avon perfume bottle swiped from his mom's bathroom. Last year, he'd gotten ahold of eleven cardboard stand-ups of Worf the Klingon and talked eleven downtown merchants into featuring them in the shops' storefront window displays. Each Worf held a sign reading TELL RAIN BERGHOFF, "HAPPY BIRTHDAY."

I'd been so embarrassed that I didn't leave home for a week. Four months later, people had still been wishing me a happy birthday.

Galen laughed, slowing his swing by dragging his shoe soles against the wood chips, and I did the same. I thought he might be cold and too much of a guy to say so. I thought maybe he was ready to head back home.

But then Galen reached inside of his shirt pocket and handed me a jewelry-sized gift box. It was wrapped in violet tissue and tied with a metallic black ribbon.

"Does it bite?" I asked, looking at him sideways.

Galen shook his head. "You see any airholes?"

I frowned. "It's not dead, is it?"

He shook his head again, innocentlike. "Nope."

"Will it publicly humiliate me in any way?"

He laughed again, this time nervously.

Suspicious, I thought. I almost asked another question, but I caught a glimpse of pink rising on his cheeks. It's just the cold, I told myself. But I could've sworn he was blushing. To the best of my memory, Galen never blushed.

Opening the box, I lifted a necklace from the puffed cotton. A black suede pouch, in the shape of a half-moon and as small as my thumbprint, lay between dangling leather ties. Seed beads in daybreak colors—crimson, yellow, and burnt orange—lined the curving seam, sealed with white crisscross stitches. Larger daybreak-colored beads flanked the pouch, bordered by even more beads—two plastic midnight blues and two scalloped metal silvers. The necklace smelled smoky, bittersweet, and granny-ancient.

I remembered seeing it last June, displayed on a Lakota trader's table at a powwow in Oklahoma City. Aunt Georgia had taken Galen and me on a road trip to visit family, and he had trailed after me down crowded aisle after aisle.

Later, with fingers sticky from an Indian taco, I'd focused my camera on a girl turning with a rose-quilted shawl. I shot her two ways, first to capture one footstep, one flying rose, and then slower to preserve the blur of her dance, the rhythm of the Drum. Meanwhile, Galen had ditched me on a popcorn run to shop.

Tying the necklace around my neck, I realized it was the furthest thing from what I'd been expecting, that it was the kind of gift a boy gets for his girl.

Leave it to Galen to be the brave one first.

His blue eyes had lost their usual mischief, and it was clear that something had changed when he looked at me. But right then, I didn't have the words, and I was pretty sure he didn't, either. So we did the only thing we could have. We began soaring again.

As the swing carried me up, I had to bite the insides of my chapped lips to keep from grinning. My toes tingled with stardust. Even if I chickened out at midnight, this let me know I could bide my time. Maybe Galen and I would be like Gramma and Grampa Scott, high-school sweethearts who'd never belong to anyone else.

I told myself that if Galen had ever looked at another girl the way he was looking at me, it had just been for practice. It absolutely didn't count.

Later, Galen shot by me on his swing, yelling, "I'm going to jump."

"You're too high," I said, trying not to sound like his mother.

Galen let go of the chains and flew, shouting, "Happy New Year!"

Snow fell like parade confetti. "Ten from the Chinese judge," Galen called, sticking the landing and raising his hands high. "Nine point five from the French."

He jogged down the hill, and Chewie circled him, tail wagging.

"A lousy eight from the American," Galen added, spinning in the soccer field with his arms outstretched. "What kind of loyalty is that?"

I heard a distant siren and the flurry of fireworks. Dragging my high-tops to slow myself, I fiddled with my camera strap. My lips itched, and my heart did a two-step.

I rose from my swing. It was happy birthday time.

Broken Star

FROM MY JOURNAL:

The KEEP OUT *sign hadn't stopped Galen, or stopped me from following him.*

Walking home from Vacation Bible School, we broke a batch of no-no's to check out the new city hall construction site. He tripped over a two-by-four and tumbled into a big ole hole, landing in a muddy puddle. A rescue attempt landed me in there, too. By the time we shimmied out, well, piglets would've been more sanitary.

Later, in my driveway, Galen told Mama, "It was my fault."

When she folded her arms and sighed, I added, "We're sorry."

In the moment that passed, I said a quick prayer for forgiveness. Then Mama laughed and opened her arms wide. "Partners in crime," she declared, drawing us close, not caring about messing up her own denim jumper. "You're still in trouble, you know."

That hug with Mama and Galen, that's my safest memory.

JANUARY 1

The ringing phone stirred me, and I stretched my legs under my broken-star quilt. I could expect Grampa Berghoff and Fynn to answer the phone, the door, and all of my whims for the rest of the day, my fourteenth birthday, the first day of this year.

Grampa drummed my door. "You up?" he asked.

My yawn landed in a smile. We had our own traditions. Birthdays meant breakfast in bed. Orange juice, blueberry pancakes, and, for dessert, a box of Cracker Jacks.

I pushed up against my canopy headboard. "Enter," I said.

For the first time, no room service. My hands curled around the edge of the quilt. If somebody didn't hurry up with breakfast, we'd be late for church. "Where, pray tell, is Our morning meal?" I demanded, pretending royal indifference. "Our orange juice, Our pancakes, Our . . ."

Grampa came in, wearing his ratty bathrobe, fuzzy slippers, and a look that had nothing to do with celebrations. "That was Mrs. Owen on the phone," he said. Grampa knelt at my bedside, and his cold hands cradled my warm ones. "This is going to be hard, but . . . I'd best just spit it out. She called to let us know that Galen passed away last night. It was an accident, Rainbow. Nobody's fault."

My eyes grew heavy, fuller, like sponges. My lips and fingertips chilled. I felt the news clear to the most locked-down places inside of me, clear to that part I thought had died years before with my mom. And that was before it began to make sense.

When Galen had left me the night before, it had already been past his curfew. He'd said it would be faster for him to run straight home than return to my house and get a ride from Fynn. Two blocks, I'd figured. No problem. What could've gone wrong?

I whispered pieces of questions, and Grampa offered parts of answers.

He explained how some bottle rockets had caught on the roof of the Tischers' barn and how the volunteer firefighters had been called out. By the time they'd headed back to the station, the streets had turned to ice.

The driver said that he never saw Galen, that Galen just ran right into the road. Even if the driver had tried to brake, with the ice, it would've been too late.

For a long while, I didn't mouth anything but the word no. Still, I knew it was true, because Grampa had told me, and if he could, Grampa would protect me from any hurt.

But I don't hurt, I told myself. Though my body was still shaking, my eyes had suddenly gone dry.

Six Months Later

FROM MY JOURNAL:

Mrs. Owen called my house twice on the day Galen died, once the next day, and three times the day before he was buried at the Garden of Roses Cemetery. She'd heard what the volunteer fire department had to say. She'd wanted to talk to me about what had happened that night and about her plans for Galen's funeral.

I refused to take the calls, and Grampa told her I wasn't ready for talking.

I'm still not.

In fact, I was the only person in town who didn't go to the funeral. My ex–second-best friend spoke in my place. Queenie read a poem she'd written for the occasion.

Fynn told me; that's how I know. I didn't ask, but it's hard not wondering what Queenie said that day.

JUNE 26

As my laptop modem trilled, Fynn declared, "You may be a virtual person, but some of us need groceries." He was sitting across the kitchen table, looking up at me from his coffee.

When I didn't answer, Fynn set down his Starfleet Academy mug and said, "Aunt Georgia called this morning.

Her grandnephew Spence is coming up to visit from Oklahoma City, so she's pushing back the start date for Indian Camp."

I couldn't believe Fynn hadn't given up. For weeks, he'd been dropping hints about my signing up for the program Aunt Georgia was coordinating. But there was no way. It wasn't that I didn't appreciate her efforts. It was just that I hadn't been out and about in a long time. I wasn't ready to start with Indian Camp.

Granted, I felt a little guilty.

Aunt Georgia had lived in Hannesburg my whole life, ever since marrying her husband, who she first met on a visit with Gramma to see then-baby Fynnegan. Their mamas, Aunt Georgia's and Gramma Scott's—my great-gramma Melba—grew up together at Seneca Indian School in Oklahoma and had stayed best friends.

Aunt Georgia had been there when Mom was born at Gramma and Grampa Scott's house in Eufaula, right there with the midwife in the bedroom. She'd been there when I was born, too, in the local base hospital.

But Indian Camp? It sounded like the kind of thing where a bunch of probably suburban, probably rich, probably white kids tromped around a woodsy park, calling themselves "princesses," "braves," or "guides."

Not my style. For that matter, not Aunt Georgia's. But the last couple of months, she'd been talking about doing this summer camp for Native kids in Hannesburg.

It sounded like some kind of bonding thing. Or maybe just bait to lure me out of the house. No, I was being full of myself. More likely, it had something to do with the way Hannesburg schools taught about Indians and, because of that, the way it sometimes felt to be an Indian in Hannesburg schools.

At school, the subject of Native Americans pretty much comes up just around Turkey Day, like those cardboard cutouts of the Pilgrims and the pumpkins and the squash taped to the windows at McDonald's. And the so-called Indians always look like bogeymen on the prairie, windblown cover boys selling paperback romances, or baby-faced refugees from the world of Precious Moments. I usually get through it by reading sci-fi fanzines behind my textbooks until we move on to Kwanza.

Being a retired science teacher, Aunt Georgia would get especially frustrated. "Too little improvement after too many years," she'd say. Not that Aunt Georgia's program was supposed to be like school. "Camp, not curriculum," was how she'd described it. The focus was going to be on science and technology, her specialties—well, the science anyway. My brother would be lending a hand on the tech angle.

Knowing full well Fynn was waiting for me to say something, I closed my empty e-mail box and opened a season-two Mulder-Scully romance fic on an X-Philes site. Fynn got me hooked on fandom. He had almost every sci-fi show archived. We were into everything after the original *Star Trek*, and we used to have these all-day marathons, watching every episode in a series or season. Lately, though, he spent all of his time with his girlfriend, Natalie.

"Rain," he added, apparently deciding my brain had been sucked into cyberspace, "that means you still have time to sign up for Indian Camp."

I read the spoiler warnings and started the story.

Hours later, I still sat at the table, painting my uneven fingernails Hot Noir and skimming the conversation in a WBTV chat room.

The highlight of my day had been receiving a postcard of the night lights of Las Vegas from Grampa Berghoff. He'd blown town earlier that week for his annual vacation.

In scratchy scribbles, the postcard read:

Dear Rainbow,
Vegas sure beats the riverboats in Kansas City. Won $300 on the slots and met a sexy widow named Clementine at the hotel's all-you-can-eat buffet.
They have eight kinds of Jell-O.
Wish me luck!
XOXO, Grampa
P.S. Take care of your brother.

Maybe Fynn is right, I thought. Maybe I need to get out more.

Splotchy clouds had softened my hometown, and afternoon sprinkles had chased people off the cracked sidewalks and pitted streets. All the better for avoiding those wreck-on-the-highway looks and the questions tucked inside of questions.

Since Galen's death, I'd quietly pushed away my choir and soccer buddies, my school counselor, and the youth pastor. Fynn and Grampa took my calls, and they turned away visitors.

Aside from Fynn's hints about Indian Camp, my family had never pushed. Eventually, other people backed off, too, and I fell out of my regular circles. But I knew folks were curious about how I was doing.

Chewie tugged on his leash, but somehow he knew better than to walk me past Burnham Elementary, the Garden of Roses Cemetery, or Galen's street.

When Chewie and I arrived at Hein's Grocery Barn, the parking lot was empty except for Bernadette Rae Mitchell's pink Cadillac.

Just then, Uncle Ed's rusting pickup rumbled up the street alongside me. He leaned out the window and called, "If it isn't my favorite rug rat!" Uncle Ed looked good. Not too pink. Not too puffy. Not since he'd gotten serious and regular about going to AA. "Doing a little shopping?" he asked.

"Thinking about it," I replied.

"That's my girl!" He saluted me and smiled, showing off his gold front tooth. It's the second gold tooth in that slot. He pawned the first one for beer money. "Take it one day and all that," he added as the truck rolled on its way.

A few steps later, I tied Chewie's leash to the bike rack and vowed to start small on my first expedition to the store in months: dog treats and a Cherry Coke.

The whoosh of the automatic doors alerted store clerk Lorelei of my arrival. Her eyebrows-high stare almost made me miss my camera. I could imagine her on the phone the minute I left: "Rain Berghoff sighting, aisle six."

Marching to Paper Products & Pet Food, I grabbed a box of hydrant-shaped dog treats and then turned up Frozen Foods. Before I knew it, Bernadette Rae had spotted me. She was resting one hand on her grocery cart and rummaging through frozen turkey pot-pies with the other. Her hair was a violet blue. A botched experiment, no doubt.

As I strolled by, Bernadette Rae gave me the once-over and said, "Your ends look a tad ragged, Rain. When's the last time you were in for a trim?"

"I'll try to stop by the salon next week," I answered, not stopping to chat.

Only Lorelei stood between me and the exit. I wondered why I'd been so tense.

That's when I found myself standing at point-blank range in front of the one person I least wanted to see. If life had been a video game, I would've exploded in Frozen Foods. As it was, I almost dropped my dog treats.

I'd spent the last few months trying not to think about Galen, only to run smack into his mother, Della Owen (Mrs. Owen, even to her grown-up friends), on my first excursion in months. She was holding a box of English tea and, as always, wearing tailored gray. Her blond hair looked professionally styled. It's common knowledge that she never lets Bernadette Rae touch it.

"Hello, Cassidy Rain," Mrs. Owen said. "I've been meaning to talk to you."

I raised one hand in a wave, trying to figure out why. I'd heard about her recent failed run for mayor, and I knew she had already begun campaigning for the rematch.

But I hadn't actually talked to Mrs. Owen since her

three phone calls to Galen on New Year's Eve.

My only consolation was that at least Mrs. Owen and I weren't alone in the grocery aisle. I mean, what could she say with Bernadette Rae still within listening range?

"Bernie," Mrs. Owen added, glancing over my shoulder, her voice cooler than anything in the freezers, "if you'll excuse us . . ."

I should've expected that.

After Bernadette Rae wheeled away, Mrs. Owen said, "Tell me about Georgia Wilhelm's Native American youth program."

That didn't faze me. Mrs. Owen had always been abrupt. And the way I had it figured, she was asking me about Indian Camp to be polite. It was something we could talk about besides Galen, and neither one of us was ready to mention his name yet.

After all, I was the last person to see her only child alive. If Galen and I hadn't gone out prowling that night, the accident never would've happened. If he hadn't been with me, Galen might still have been alive.

"It's a camp, like a summer camp," I answered. "That's all I know."

"Surely you'll be participating?" she asked.

"No, ma'am," I replied, trying to come up with something safe to say.

No use.

"Got to run now," I finally announced, taking a few steps around her. "Dinner."

It was only about two o'clock in the afternoon.

"Chewie's dinner, I mean." I jiggled my dog treats,

adding, "He's waiting for me outside. Big dog. Big appetite."

I took off before I could make a bigger fool out of myself.

At the checkout, I grabbed a plastic bottle of Cherry Coke from the minifridge next to the magazines and set it behind my dog treats on Lorelei's counter.

Between her bleached bangs and Salvation Army outfit—a checked halter top and faded cutoffs—she looked the part of her reputation. Around town, folks call her "the Lorelei Express," and not because she's fast at the cash register. Fynn had actually dated her, back when they were juniors in high school.

"Paper or plastic?" she asked, scanning the bar codes.

"Neither," I answered, handing her a five.

Lorelei tapped register keys and said, "I hear Fynn and the new girl are serious."

After shoving the receipt in my back pocket, I replied, "I guess."

"The new girl" she'd mentioned was Natalie, who'd first arrived in town last fall to work as the news editor for the *Hannesburg Weekly Examiner*.

Last December, Natalie had moved into my brother's room, and they'd become "the couple to watch."

JUNE 27

"It's a beautiful eighty degrees today here at Andersen Air Force Base," Dad informed me, just like he did practically every time we spoke on the phone. Of course, it's always about eighty degrees in Guam.

That's his idea of hilarious.

Three years ago, the local air force base closed. Grampa Berghoff took early retirement, and Dad was transferred to South Korea (before Guam). At the time, we'd all agreed it would be best if Grampa rented out his house and moved in with us. I stayed in Hannesburg with him and Fynn, who was a commuter student at the University of Kansas.

Dad went on: "Your uncle Ed said he saw you out walking Chewie."

I nodded, even though Dad couldn't see me lying belly-down on my bed. "We both needed the exercise," I said.

"Exercised your camera lately?" he asked. "Before Grampa took off, he was telling me how much he misses working with you in the darkroom."

I glanced at my camera, hanging from the back of the wicker chair next to my hope chest. "Dad," I asked, trying to distract him, "want to talk to Natalie or Fynn?"

The line fell quiet a moment, and Dad replied, "What do you really think of that girl, that Natalie? You think she's all right?"

"Sure," I answered, trading good-byes, love-yous, and telling him to watch out for snakes. Just as I was about to hang up, Dad asked to speak with that girl himself.

My Not-So-Secret Secret Identity

FROM MY JOURNAL:

Rain is not my Indian name, not the way people think of Indian names. But I am an Indian, and it is the name my parents gave me.

They met for the first time at Bierfest, during one doozy of a thunderstorm.

Mom used to call Dad her "rainy day love."

Mom had been into nicknames. She'd dubbed our family her "patchwork tribe." I'm Muscogee Creek-Cherokee and Scots-Irish on Mom's side, Irish-German-Ojibway on Dad's. Our Ojibway blood came from Gramma Berghoff, from her father's people up in Michigan. Saginaw Chippewa.

Not that Dad talks about it. I'm told that even Gramma Berghoff, who died the year before I was born, called herself "just Irish" or "black Irish" every day of her life.

JUNE 28

Two days after my adventure at the grocery store, rain rattled gutters and tapped the roof. If it had been a school day, I would've caught my share of weather jokes. I'd kept busy dusting every room in the house and was finishing up with Dad and Mom's.

Mom had first left Eufaula, Oklahoma, for Lawrence, Kansas, to study at Haskell, a school for Indians. Sometimes I wondered what Mom had dreamed of doing with her life back then. She'd had a cousin who did paperwork for the state of Oklahoma, a cousin who did paperwork for Indian Health Service, and a cousin who did paperwork for the Bureau of Indian Affairs. Aunt Louise was a nurse. Uncle Leonard had worked a couple of years for the tribe, but by then, he was already driving a school bus. My grandparents earned their paychecks at Southwestern Bell.

Mom left Haskell after her first semester, just before she married my dad.

I touched her traditional tear dress. "Settlers' cotton," I remembered Mom saying, "torn in long strips." A padded hanger on a brass hook held the long red calico, and its skirt fanned on the antique white wall.

When she'd first hung up the dress, there had been a ribbon to fix. It was only supposed to have been there a day or two. But Mom's time had run out.

Now the dress looked wrong somehow, more like a museum piece than part of living. I hated that, but I didn't want to change anything without checking first with Dad.

It's been six years since my mother died.

As I put away my feather duster, thunder warned me that the storm had turned electrical. I noticed then that my grocery receipt was littering the kitchen table. Realizing the last thing I needed was one of Fynn's lectures about fiscal responsibility, I unplugged my laptop computer and double-clicked the Quicken icon. After keying in $4.67, I skimmed our financial records. The last time I'd bought myself anything, including film, was my black fingernail polish on Valentine's Day.

Beneath Grampa's fifteen-dollar deduction for my weekly allowance, I spotted a payment to Mrs. Georgia Wilhelm, seven bucks for Indian Camp (categorized as a "miscellaneous family expense"). The check had been written by my brother.

Through the window screens, I heard his Jeep door slam and then a round of hoots, hollers, and whistles. I didn't even have to look. The Hannesburg High junior varsity cheerleaders regularly cruise by the house to gawk at Fynn. In their Fighting Harvesters black-and-gold uniforms, they look like a six-pack of bumblebees. The fact that we live on a dead-end street makes it even more pathetic.

I suffer in comparison to my heartthrob brother. Here I am, average height, average weight, with bottle-cap boobs and eyes pinched at the corners. Nobody's impressed that I can look out the window and get a tan. Thanks to UV rays, the sun-kissed look is out.

Only my mom had admired my so-called Kansas coloring. She used to say that my hair looked like waving wheat and my eyes changed color with the weather.

Dishwater hair, I've always thought. Hazel eyes. I'm not the poetic type.

My brother is the one who inherited Mom's striking looks. Everybody besides him appreciates it, especially Natalie, Lorelei, and the pom-pom crowd.

A slightly soggy Fynn strolled into the kitchen, carrying four plastic grocery bags in each hand. One last whistle flew through the window into the kitchen.

A waste of time. Everybody knew he belonged to Natalie.

"Well," I said, tucking in a grin, "if it isn't Native American Fabio."

"For that," he answered, in what had become his trademark quote, "you should be grounded, but it would be redundant."

"You can say that again . . . and again," I answered.

Fynn plopped the groceries onto the counter, ran a hand through his damp hair, and announced, "The news from the outside world is that I had a meeting upstate today with a new client, a Kickapoo blues band called Not Your Wild West Show. They hired me to design a promotional site, you know, where they can announce upcoming gigs and sell CDs. Nice bunch of guys."

"They any good?" I asked.

Fynn slipped off his navy jacket, folded it over a chair, and replied, "Not particularly."

Lately, my brother had seemed like a different guy. In the past couple of months, he'd gotten a Jayhawk tattoo on his shoulder and then gone corporate. Good-bye shoulder-length locks, 501s, and marathon T-shirts. Hello IBM haircut, pinstripes, and Jerry Garcia ties. I wasn't sure why.

I closed the laptop and announced, "I saw the payment for Indian Camp."

As Fynn began restocking the kitchen, he said, "For dinner, we could hit Clifford's Chinese Kitchen. It's been months since your last *moo shu* fix."

I thought about it. My favorite dinner at my favorite restaurant on grocery day? In Lawrence? I wasn't even helping him unload the food. Besides, Fynn hadn't answered my question. My fingertips drummed the table, and I answered, "You hate Chinese."

"Hate? Did you say 'hate'?" Fynn's voice warbled like a southern TV preacher's. "Why, baby sister, I'd never, and I say *never,* discriminate against a community of food. That, I say, now *that,* you must believe."

He was definitely up to something.

I rose to wash the dishes, waiting.

"You know," Fynn finally said, "Aunt Georgia's Indian Camp has a real science-technology slant. She recruited me to teach Web design."

It wasn't the first time he'd mentioned it. I rinsed out his mug and reminded him, "I already know Web design."

Last fall, Fynn had taught Galen and me. We'd made a New Year's resolution to build a website. Lately, I'd thought about launching one of my own, but the idea just didn't feel right. Not without Galen.

Fynn shoved a bag of bagels into the bread box, grabbed a dishrag, and said, "I mailed the check in case you changed your mind. I thought maybe . . ."

"We're talking about two weeks," I explained, scrubbing a salad plate, trying to make him understand. "I have to weed the lawn, walk Chewie, clean the house, and . . . so on."

"Hospitals are less antiseptic," Fynn replied, drying the cutting board.

"You're so"—I shut off the faucet—"presumptuous."

It was the word I'd missed in the semifinal round of my fourth-grade spelling bee. It's been my word of choice ever since.

He had a point, though. The house had never gleamed so much, especially taking into account how I used to be on the messy side. And how Fynn had always embraced the messy side, at least pre-Natalie. And how Grampa, who prided himself on being the one to look after such things, was out of town.

I realized that hiding out had become boring, that I longed for some sunshine. A person could get only so much satisfaction out of making the world lemon-fresh.

When the doorbell buzzed, Fynn tossed his towel on the counter. He said, "That's probably Aunt Georgia."

As usual, she let herself in, dumped her leather backpack on the table, and traded a round of hugs. Since her last visit, Aunt Georgia had dyed her short graying black hair a tomato red. From a distance, nobody would have guessed she was a Muscogee Creek-Cherokee. Or, for that matter, a natural redhead.

I wasn't too surprised. Bernadette Rae had a tendency to get creative with her salon clients. But even so, Aunt Georgia's new hue was really something.

After pouring her a glass of iced tea, Fynn excused himself to work in his Domain, a home office that used to be our freestanding garage. On the way out, he said, "By the way, Rain won't be able to make it to Indian Camp."

I was worried about having hurt Aunt Georgia's feelings or having shown disrespect. But before I could say anything, she reached into her backpack and pulled out a journal with a crescent moon on the cover. "I picked up a few of these on sale," she told me, sliding it across the table. "You used to like to write."

I thanked her and turned the journal over in my hands. I had liked to write, especially in fifth and sixth grades, before photography went from a hobby to an obsession.

"I'd best get a move on," Aunt Georgia announced, downing the last of her iced tea. "My aqua aerobics class starts in ten minutes. I just dropped by to say hi." She bent and kissed my forehead. "If you do change your mind about Indian Camp, you're always welcome. But if I don't see you again before then, I expect we'll all get together over the Fourth of July."

The holiday had sneaked up on me. My toes tingled. Aunt Georgia turned away too soon to notice my surprise.

As the door shut behind her, I thought about how much time had gone by since Galen had died. It had been six months already. Six months. The Fourth of July would've been his birthday, an occasion I'd sworn to always celebrate.

I shuffled like a zombie into my room, opened my hope chest, and took out the box with my birthday necklace inside. It had been sitting on a stack of unanswered cards and letters from my grandparents in Oklahoma. Before going to bed that last night, I'd taken the necklace off so as not to get it tangled in my hair.

I wasn't ready to wear it again, not yet. I wanted to

keep it as one last secret between Galen and me. Despite everything—his notorious taste in presents, it being his last night on the planet—he'd still managed to give me something that I'd always treasure for my holiday birthday.

I decided that somehow I had to keep my end of the deal and honor his.

The big question was how. I'd hardly whispered Galen's name since the last New Year's Day, and his birthday—the Fourth of July—was only a week away.

Moo Shu and Peace

FROM MY JOURNAL:

Last autumn, the day before the dance, Galen had said, "I'm taking Queenie."

"Like a date?" I asked, joining him on my creaking porch swing.

Galen explained, "We've been going together for a while. I would've told you, but we decided not to tell anybody. You know how people talk."

I'd never admitted to Queenie or anyone else that I liked him *liked him.*

Galen's bangs fell forward. "Would you go out with a black person?" he asked.

Somewhere in my memory, I'd been told it was okay to be friends with black people, but not more than friends. "I guess," I answered. "Worried about your mom?"

Mrs. Owen's rule had been "no dating until high school."

"I'll deal with Mother," he'd said. "It's my life."

JUNE 28

While Natalie propped her dripping happy-face umbrella on the porch, Fynn lugged in a red paper bag. Under the dragon logo, it read CLIFFORD'S CHINESE KITCHEN.

"Special delivery," he announced.

"We come bearing *moo shu* veggies with hot-and-sour soup," Natalie added, scratching behind Chewie's ears. "Your favorites."

The takeout was a peace offering.

I'm a devout believer in *moo shu* and peace.

While Natalie and Fynn unpacked the food on the coffee table, I muted the TV and plopped couch pillows on the hardwood floor. Natalie lit a blue candle, and her single silver hoop earring caught the flame.

Grampa teases Natalie that she looks like a china doll and dresses like a lumberjack. He's right. She wears hiking boots and overalls with flannel shirts in cold weather and with T-shirts in warm. Her close-cropped blond hair sticks out in all directions. Usually, her only jewelry is the earring. Lately, shadows have circled her gray eyes.

The blue candle smelled like vanilla, mingling with the aromas of my hot-and-sour soup and *moo shu* veggies, Fynn's egg-drop soup and *kung pao* chicken, as well as Natalie's steaming wonton soup and garlic shrimp.

That last order stumped me. Natalie is Hannesburg's only known vegetarian. (It's less annoying because she's also the only member of our household who really knows how to cook.) When I asked about the carnivorder, Natalie said she'd decided to expand her diet to include seafood, eggs, and milk, so she wouldn't always have to drive clear to Lawrence for takeout.

Chewie hunkered beneath the coffee table, waiting for scraps.

I'd almost finished my dinner when Fynn reached over

and fondled Natalie's pirate earring. He hadn't eaten a spoonful of his egg-drop soup, let alone a bite of his main course, or mine or Natalie's. Fynn never ignores food.

I clicked my chopsticks and asked, "On a diet, Fynnegan?"

My resident love doves traded a look. Natalie pushed back her plate. Fynn grabbed the dog-gnawed remote and clicked off a special report about the president.

"We've been trying to tell you all week," Natalie said. "We're engaged."

"To be married," Fynn added, reaching beneath the table to pet Chewie.

What could I say? I jumped up to hug them both, and my elbow bumped the container of Natalie's lukewarm wonton soup. It gushed over the table, and Chewie slurped it like only a big dog could. Somehow, the flickering candle survived.

Once we'd mopped the mess, Natalie spilled the details. She'd proposed to Fynn at Potter Lake with a bouquet of sunflowers. Her mother wanted a formal wedding at Good Shepherd Episcopal Church and a sit-down reception at some golf-course country club in Overland Park, but Fynn and Natalie planned to get married in three weeks at First Baptist in Hannesburg. Small wedding. Sheet cake and fruit punch reception in the church basement. Fynn had already told Aunt Georgia, Uncle Ed, Gramma and Grampa Scott, and Grampa Berghoff. Dad had already requested leave to fly home from Guam.

"So I'm not exactly the first to know?" I asked, keeping my voice light.

Natalie fiddled with her earring.

"It's my fault," Fynn said. "I told her I'd tell you."

I tapped my plate with my chopsticks, prompting him with an "And?"

Fynn held a chunk of *kung pao* chicken to my lips and said, "I chickened out."

I bit into the spicy offering. Fynn isn't the chicken type. Or the spicy type, for that matter. He'd been the only one at the table eating with a fork.

Natalie grabbed the *Examiner* and pointed me to "Engagements." The entry read:

> *Mr. and Mrs. Lucas Lewis of Overland Park announce the engagement of their daughter, Natalie Michelle, to Mr. Fynnegan Patrick Berghoff, son of Maj. Erik P. Berghoff and his late wife, of Hannesburg. Ms. Lewis, a member of Alpha Delta Pi sorority, is a graduate of the University of Kansas and the news editor of the* Examiner. *Mr. Berghoff, also a KU graduate, is a computer consultant and a website designer.*

Natalie should have used Mom's whole name, not that I mentioned it.

"I had no idea you were in a sorority," I said.

"I moved out after my first semester," she explained, glancing at me sideways. "My mother made me put it in anyway."

Natalie's mother is a PR exec for Hallmark, and her dad is an accountant at Sprint. They live about a half hour east in Johnson County, a Kansas City suburb where shopping malls are considered sacred, parking is plentiful, the tallest tree is five years old, and every other restaurant serves fried cheese.

"What's this?" Fynn asked, raising the editorial page.

Natalie leaned over to see what he was talking about and said, "I guess Mrs. Owen figures that if she keeps chipping, she'll beat our esteemed mayor the next time around."

Fynn appeared to be rereading whatever had upset him. I doubted Fynn paid much more attention to local politics than I did, at least beyond handing out flyers to support Uncle Ed's bid for city council. He'd called the last elections "glorified family feuds" and said it was no accident they fell during April, "the month of fools."

Fynn closed and folded the newspaper, like it had offended him somehow.

Natalie set down her chopsticks and said, "You know, Fynn, the letter does mention that she has the highest respect . . ."

The flame wavered, and Fynn muttered, "How politically correct." He waved the paper at her and asked, "You approve of this?"

"It's the editorial page," Natalie answered, sounding like a journalism professor. "It's for what anybody thinks whether you or I agree with them or not."

An engaged couple should've been getting along better. Not that anyone was asking what I thought. Retreat sounded like a good idea.

I tossed the empty take-out containers and still-wrapped fortune cookies into the Clifford's bag, grabbed the *Examiner* from Fynn, and marched down the hall to my bedroom with Chewie.

Fynn called, "Rain, stay out of it."

I shut the door behind my dog and opened the *Examiner* to "Letters to the Editor." The only published letter read:

Dear Editor,

Next week's city council agenda indicates a $1,340 request in conjunction with a Native American summer youth camp program here in Hannesburg.

As a fiscally responsible citizen, I have no choice but to voice my objection. Please understand that I have the highest respect for both Native American culture and Mrs. Georgia Wilhelm, the program coordinator. On an informal basis, I even encouraged my own child to accompany her to Native American events.

But is it the place of our city to finance a special program that serves only one small ethnic group? It merits noting that one of the young teens is an out-of-towner. While it has been verified that his parents would finance his portion of the expenses, his outsider status only underscores the minuscule participation number of four.

Furthermore, I have verified that the only local Native American child who's an honor roll student is not on the participation roster. If she does not find this activity worthy of her time, why should we find it worthy of our tax dollars?

Sincerely,
Mrs. Della Owen

I flipped to page six. Sure enough, the city council agenda read:

II. New Business
A. Financing Request: $1,340, American Indian Youth Summer Camp.
Georgia A. Wilhelm, coordinator.

I couldn't believe it. Neon Idiot Me had stood right there, holding my dog treats in Frozen Foods, and had told Mrs. Owen that I was blowing off Aunt Georgia's Indian Camp. Mrs. Owen used that news flash to counter Aunt Georgia's financing request, probably just to make Mayor Tahiti Rummel look bad.

Bottom line: Mrs. Owen needed voters for round two of her run for mayor, Aunt Georgia needed money for Indian Camp, and my big mouth had stuck me in the middle.

If I did nothing, it would look like I was siding with Mrs. Owen. If I joined Indian Camp, it would look like Aunt Georgia had pressured me—something she'd never do. Besides, the way I saw it, my heritage was not something to be talked about in the weekly news.

To think Fynn wondered why I never left the house.

The bathroom smelled like honey and cucumber. Natalie stood in front of the steam-clouded mirror, wearing a green herbal face mask.

"So Indian Camp is news," I said. "Multicultural news."

Natalie's frown cracked her drying mask. "Hadn't thought of that," she replied.

It surprised me to hear her say so. Natalie is always looking for stories, and she talks a lot about how newspapers should cover, as she puts it, "the increasingly diverse population." That's a monster challenge in Hannesburg. My hometown has about two thousand German-Americans and assorted other white people, three Native families, one black family, and one Indian-American family (as in from India, although they moved here from Garden City, Kansas).

Lately, Natalie had been toiling seventy-hour weeks on the Independence Day tabloid while almost single-handedly cranking out the regular weekly paper.

Luckily, she'd recently hired some temporary help. The *Examiner* can't afford to pay its interns much more than minimum wage, but every semester a couple of journalism students show up for the experience, a letter of recommendation, and a chance to build their string books and clip portfolios. Some guy named "the Flash" was her latest indentured servant, a reporting intern who was going to be a sophomore at KU. Fynn had called him "a trip," but I hadn't met the guy yet.

Natalie flipped on the cold water. "I'm desperate," she said. "All I have lined up for the issue after the Fourth of July tab is the regular meetings. You know, merchants' association, city council."

I tried to cheer her up. "Maybe Butcher Slotnick's hogs will get loose and chase Sheriff Appelt down Lincoln Avenue again. Or one of Mrs. Washington's breeding ostriches will take a peck at another unsuspecting jogger. Or, if you're really blessed, Joey Michaels will spot another Jesus face in his Cool Whip."

"We can only pray," Natalie answered, splashing her face.

Suddenly, inspiration struck. "If it would help," I said, "I could shoot Indian Camp. Just a day would do it."

"Art!" Natalie exclaimed, straightening, splotches of green goop sticking to her dripping face. "Do you have any idea how gray the front page will look with no art?"

At the last minute, her photojournalism intern had bagged the *Examiner* for a better paying, big-time summer job at the *Wichita Eagle*. Bad news for Natalie. The *Examiner*'s budget was tight, and she had been counting on a staff shooter for summer.

Natalie splashed off what was left of her facial mask and patted a hand towel on her cheeks. "Okay," she said, "but it's the Flash's story, and your pictures have to be professional. No setups. Something decent, or I won't run it."

Natalie had run family travel photos shot with a disposable. I smiled at the thought that her standards were higher for me.

"But look," she added, "we both know Fynn wants you to join the program. If you change your mind and go ahead, that'll be a conflict of interest." Natalie said "conflict of interest" like it was the eighth deadly sin. "That means you're too close to the story to cover it," she explained, "and the deal is off."

"No problem," I replied, shaking her hand.

Mrs. Burnham, who sells advertising space for the

Examiner, had dated Uncle Ed between Aunt Carol and Aunt Noreen, between gold tooth number one and gold tooth number two. If I asked, she'd spread the word that I was covering Indian Camp. She'd even explain that Natalie had told me I couldn't both shoot the story and participate. If people wanted to talk about Mrs. Owen challenging Aunt Georgia's financing request, they would just have to leave me out of it.

⚘ Indian Camp

FROM MY JOURNAL:

Last fall, two hours before the dance, Galen had shuffled up my front walk. "Queenie and I broke up," he said. "She's going to the party with Ernie Blastingbaum."

Ernie had been her partner for a school report about water waste. It was during Queenie's environmental phase. Queenie always obsesses in phases, but dumping Galen for her sewage partner? Please.

The next Monday at school, Queenie had greeted me by saying, "What do you know?"

I'd opened our shared locker and dumped her pink tampon box, her color-coded notebooks, and her tabbed textbooks onto the eighth-grade hallway's floor. "Queenie Deloris Washington," I said, "you're going to have to find a new locker partner."

JUNE 29

The first morning of Indian Camp, I met the Flash at the entrance to D. P. Tischer Park. He was wearing a nose ring and a black trench coat. Fynn had told me the Flash supposedly always carried a flask of tequila in one of its inner pockets.

According to Natalie, the Flash's real name was Jordan

Guller, nicknamed "the Flasher" by his pledge brothers because of the coat. He'd shortened it to "the Flash" on homecoming weekend of his freshman year, when his parents came to visit.

I was relieved to see the T-shirt peeking from the neck of the coat and the faded jeans that covered his lower half. My life was complicated enough without throwing in a seminaked college boy from St. Louis.

"My photographer," the Flash said. "And I thought *I* lacked experience."

Ignoring him, I spotted Aunt Georgia's tomato-red hair. She was one of five people seated in a circle beneath a tree across the park. "There," I said, pointing. "Now all I have to do is ask them whether I can shoot the story."

"Ask?" the Flash repeated. "We're talking about a publicly funded program on public property."

It seemed disrespectful to barge in with camera ready, and I hoped that Natalie had remembered to call Aunt Georgia earlier that morning. Natalie used to click off her list of things to do, but lately she hadn't been herself.

"Why?" the Flash asked, glancing at my camera. "Will they think you're trying to steal their souls or something?"

It required a supreme effort, but I decided to be the professional one, so I kept my mouth shut. The Flash followed me, and our footsteps sank into the soggy grass.

As the Flash and I drew closer, Spence grinned at me. I'd heard Aunt Georgia speak of him now and then. The son of lawyers with an in-ground pool in their suburban backyard. A tad round for a Gap ad, though he dressed for the job. Played baseball. Into computers. He could've passed for a full-blood if it weren't for his startling green eyes. The only reason Spence and I hadn't met already was that he'd been staying with his Osage grandparents in Pawhuska last summer when Aunt Georgia, Galen, and I had gone down to Okie City.

Twins Dmitri and Marie Headbird had kicked off their sandals and placed them side by side in the grass. They were two of the local Native teenagers Mrs. Owen had mentioned in her letter to the editor.

Queenie looked up, studying the Flash. I had no idea what she was doing at Indian Camp. Since I'd last seen her, Queenie had traded in her smoothed-under bob for a braid circling the top of her head. As far as I could tell, nothing else had changed. In the sunlight, Queenie's skin looked almost the same warm tone as Aunt Georgia's. But last time I'd checked, she wasn't Native. It was a well-known fact that Queenie was the only black girl in town.

While Aunt Georgia handled introductions, Queenie didn't even try a "What do you know?"—her standard hello. She seemed surprised to see me.

Wasting no time on manners, the Flash announced, "We're here for the *Examiner* to do a story on your"—he checked his notes—"Native American summer youth camp."

"If that's okay," I added.

Marie dug into the pocket of her lilac sundress for a Snoopy Pez dispenser. When she pulled back the plastic beagle's head, candy slid forward. "Want one?" she asked.

I accepted, glancing at her brother. Despite Dmitri's slender build, somehow his T-shirt with the Superman logo suited him. Maybe it was the way a stray lock of dark hair fell on his forehead. Or the Clark Kent glasses.

"Would we get our pictures in the paper?" he asked.

"If I can manage something decent," I said.

The Flash explained, "We're going to listen in, ask a few questions. . . ."

Queenie picked a dandelion. Dmitri lifted a ladybug with his index finger. Spence popped a bubble, and Marie scooted closer to Aunt Georgia.

The Flash began again: "So if it's all right with you . . ."

"Why of course," Aunt Georgia said. "Everything's just fine."

It was time to get to work.

Moving so the tree trunk would block the sun from directly striking my lens, I tried one angle after another and fretted about losing details to the short, dense shadows.

Aunt Georgia reached into her backpack for a fistful of blue pens and four matching journals, just like mine. She gave them to the Indian Campers and invited them to write poems, essays, stories, and random thoughts. She said, "Rain's big brother, Fynn, will be showing us how to work up a website." Aunt Georgia gestured toward the Headbirds. "Dmitri and Marie's big brother, Ron, is waiting tables this summer at Tricia's Barbecue House, but he'll be joining us for those sessions."

So there would eventually be another Indian Camper. Mrs. Owen hadn't known about Ron when she'd written her letter to the editor. Of course, I thought, she didn't know everything. For some reason, I found that a comfort.

"Right now," Aunt Georgia added, "we need to think

about creating some content to put on the site. It'd sure be nice to include some of your writing."

Spence's eyes widened, and my camera caught him shutting his journal.

"Volunteers only," Aunt Georgia added.

"Do we need drawings?" Dmitri asked.

Aunt Georgia assured him that drawings were welcome and then reached into her backpack again. She retrieved a handful of granola bars and tossed one to everyone, including me.

The Flash returned his and said, "No thanks." When she pulled out seven boxes of Hi-C, the Flash again declined. He stepped away from the group for a moment to jog back to the park's welcome sign. He apparently wanted to double-check its official name.

Kind of hyper, I thought. But maybe that made for a good reporter.

"What do you think of him?" Queenie whispered to Marie. "Cute, huh?"

"I think he's going to pass out," Marie said, sipping her juice. "It's too hot for that outfit."

"What do you think of me?" Spence pitched in with a winning smile.

"Not much," Queenie answered, and Marie seemed to hold back her own grin.

Dmitri stayed out of it, but I recognized the protective look on his face and the way his shoulders straightened. Fynn is the same way on those rare occasions when a boy happens to pay the slightest attention to me.

"Rain," Aunt Georgia began, "how's Natalie?"

I tried to keep the concern out of my voice. It would've been okay to tell her I was worried about the fight between Fynn and Natalie, but not with Queenie and three strangers in listening range. "She's fine," I mumbled. "Working a lot."

The tone of my voice seemed to dampen everyone's mood. The group was quiet for a moment, and then the Flash returned.

At that point, Aunt Georgia began speaking again. "What I'm hoping," she said, "is that once the crop is ready, we'll be renting a minivan and taking a road trip to the Leech Lake Reservation in Minnesota so you kids can be there when it's time to harvest the rice. Dmitri and Marie's grandparents have invited us to visit."

Not wanting to look at Aunt Georgia, I weighed my tank of a Nikon in my hands, running a fingertip over the dents and dings where the black paint had been chipped. I couldn't say the idea wasn't tempting, a road trip to Ojibway country.

And I was sure that even though she wasn't showing it, Aunt Georgia was disappointed that I wouldn't be coming along. She knew my family as well as I did, knew about my own Ojibway heritage. Even with Dmitri and Marie being part of Indian Camp, that particular destination didn't feel like a coincidence. Mom had always said to consider new opportunities carefully, even if they might make me uncomfortable at first.

For once, I tried not to think about her words.

Malibu Pocahontas

FROM MY JOURNAL:

Third grade. Mrs. Taylor's class. The assignment was to dress up as an important person and give a report about that person to the class. Two sources. I got it in my head that I wanted to pick an Indian woman, and a trip to the library narrowed my choices to Sacajawea or Pocahontas.

I chose former Kansas senator Nancy Kassebaum instead.

JUNE 29

I don't remember ever not wanting to be a photographer. When I was four or five years old, Grampa bought me a toy camera, and I carried it like a baby blanket.

By the time I'd turned ten, I was borrowing his Minolta.

By age twelve, I'd started scraping my money together to buy a 35-mm of my own. For weeks, I'd scoured shutterbug magazines for a good deal and pumped up my fund of allowance and birthday money by mowing lawns. At $250, the Nikon I chose was a steal, but the costs kept on coming—printing paper, lenses, a flash.

Grampa helped out, showed me how to shoot, and let me use his darkroom. He taught me how to see like a real photographer—details, texture, light and shadows.

Without him, I'd probably still be using automatics.

When I walked into the *Examiner*'s darkroom, I couldn't help comparing it with Grampa Berghoff's and mine in the attic.

At home, black plastic sheeting covered the window to block out daylight. A red safelight hung over the three developing trays that rested on a sheet of plywood propped over the bathtub. The enlarger sat on the counter next to the sink, where we washed prints.

Crowded but homey.

The musty darkroom at the *Hannesburg Weekly Examiner* was like a giant walk-in closet with a double sink. It had all the essentials, plus old photos of floods, fires, and fireworks. Chemicals had long stained the concrete floor.

It was spacious, uncharted territory. Glorious.

Grampa always says a darkroom is like a magic cave, low on light, smelly. A different adventure for every shooter, every time. A place of possibilities. Using filters, papers, and chemical mixes, the photographer can reproduce, rediscover, and reinvent realities.

Most of my first roll had been shot before that afternoon—the Christmas lights I'd taken six months earlier, after visiting the playground with Galen and Chewie. I'd used fence posts, mailboxes, and car hoods to substitute for a tripod, and my filter had created starburst effects. My favorite showed off the shimmer of the giant wire flamingo strung with holiday lights on the mayor's front lawn. Along the way, I'd taken four shots of Galen, just to tease him, calling him a "supermodel." The moon hadn't been bright enough to make those pictures come out. Sure enough, those frames looked empty.

Vacant.

Negatives show scenes in reversed light. Mine showed too many snapshots and not enough pictures of the Indian Campers at the park. At first, I'd jabbed the shutter release button instead of squeezing it, blurring the images. Halfway through, I'd realized telephone wires cluttered my shots. In the next two negatives, waving water from the in-ground sprinklers appeared to spurt out of Marie's head and shoulders. In another frame, I'd decapitated Queenie.

Nerves, I guess.

After a few hours, I sloshed yet another blank sheet of paper in the developer and waited as the image slowly emerged. I'd managed to shoot only one decent photo. The Indian Campers all seemed in sync—Dmitri and Marie without their shoes, Spence blowing a bubble, Queenie with her regal braid, and Aunt Georgia with her backpack.

The scene almost made me wish I wasn't addicted to black-and-white film. But Grampa always says that true artists shoot the highlights and the shadows because stories live in shades of gray. He says color can hide the truth.

Finally, I pulled the paper out of the developer, let it drip, and dropped it into the fixer. It had taken eight prints to get it right.

After my final effort dried, I stepped out and let myself savor working in a real-life newsroom: the cheap wood paneling, the industrial tile, the agricultural calendar from the local insurance office. The place smelled like worn boots, stale cigarettes, and burning wax. Mrs. Burnham looked up from the ad she was designing to tell me Natalie had stepped out for a doctor's appointment. Mrs. Grubert snagged the phone at the front desk.

The Flash hunched in front of a Mac, eating Oreo cookies the wrong way, like sandwiches. "Any luck?" he asked.

I handed over the picture, telling myself I didn't care what he thought. I mean, how smart is a guy who wears a black trench coat in eighty-plus-degree weather? Marie had been right at the park. It sounded like an invitation to heatstroke.

Studying the photo, the Flash said, "Not bad, for Little Miss Ask Permission."

"You charmed Aunt Georgia," I said.

"Like a snake," he replied. The Flash licked his fingers, crumpled his cookie wrapper, aimed for the trash can, and missed. "But it was you she was glad to see."

I wondered what all Natalie had told him about me.

"Let's see," the Flash continued. "Spence lives in some place called Edmond, just outside of Oklahoma City. That leaves only three Native Americans actually from Hannesburg. Wait—do you know if the Headbirds' parents both live here in town?"

A painted hangnail had split from my right pinkie. I flicked it with my thumb and asked, "What difference does it make?"

"It's for the story," the Flash replied. "You know, 'who,

what, when, where, how, and why' under the ever-popular category of 'who.'"

Sounded more like "how many" to me. The preschool song about counting "little Indians" popped into my head. I've always hated that song. "I know of nine Indians living in town," I said.

"They prefer 'Native Americans,'" the Flash told me.

I shoved the tune out of my head and shifted my camera strap.

He jotted down the number. "I'll call Mrs. Wilhelm to double-check."

"Excuse me?" I asked.

"Look, I know you're from here," the Flash said, "and everybody seems to know too much about each other in this creepy little town. But if Nat has to run a correction, she'll shish kebab me. Your future sister-in-law is my only professional rec."

Part of the deal with being a mixed-blood is that every now and then I feel like I have to announce it. "What are you?" people sometimes ask Fynn. It sounds like they want him to ID his entire species. Because my coloring is lighter, I usually get the next standard questions: "How much Indian are you?" (About forty-five pounds' worth.) And "Are you legally [or a card-carrying] Indian?" (Yes, but only on my mother's side.)

I don't mind as much when it's Native people asking, probably because they show respect for the tribal affiliation, for my family. They never follow up with something like "You don't seem Indian to me."

I've never asked about the phrase "seem Indian," but I

figure it involves construction-paper feathers, a plastic paint pony, and Malibu Pocahontas.

Right then, I missed Galen even more than usual. He used to go everywhere with me. If I ever felt uncomfortable, he'd step up with the smooth thing to say, make a joke.

Standing in the newsroom, I didn't feel ready to deal with someone new. I wanted to hightail it back home to Fynn and Natalie, to wait for Grampa Berghoff to come home from Vegas. I wanted to do mindless, monotonous things like vacuum and dust.

"Look," I finally told the Flash, "I should know how many Indians live in Hannesburg. It's not that big of a town, and I'm one of them. Me, my brother, my uncle, Aunt Georgia, and the Headbirds."

Come to think of it, the Headbirds' moving to town had more than doubled our Native population. I'd always been the only Indian near my age who'd attended Hannesburg Middle School, prayed at the First Baptist Church, and gobbled fries at the local McDonald's. Maybe that sounds lonely, and I guess in some ways it was. But I was used to it. And besides, it wasn't like I couldn't have non-Indian friends. At least, I used to.

I glanced at the Flash.

Some people size up mixed-race kids like we're the latest models in experimental genetics. Most normal, sane, polite people at least try to look like they aren't staring. Not the Flash—he was going for it. Bug-eyed and proud. It struck me as funny—ridiculous funny, not ha-ha funny—but my smile felt tight.

I was still waiting for a question.

The Flash shifted his gaze from me to his notes, twisted back around, and keyed in a quote. He bit into another Oreo cookie, again like a sandwich.

So much for my theories on human behavior.

I decided to change the subject. "I know it's not any of my business," I said, sitting on the corner of his desk, "but is it true that you always carry tequila?"

The Flash reached into an inner pocket of his trench coat, pulled out a monogrammed silver flask, and set it on the desk. "Want some?" he asked.

I picked it up, unscrewed the cap, and asked, "Had this batch long?"

"Ages," the Flash answered. Then his expression changed from know-it-all to caught red-handed. "Why?"

Something about his questioning tone reminded me of the way Fynn had reacted as a sophomore in college when I'd asked him why he'd been carrying the same condom in his wallet for six years.

I sniffed the flask, and the smell of the tequila burned the back of my throat.

"It's full," I said.

"Image," he explained, blushing, "and emergencies."

Fynn had said pretty much the same thing.

I thought about how Uncle Ed had tried to forget Vietnam and ended up with two ex-wives to forget, too. But Fynn and Grampa had a few beers every now and then, and they didn't seem worse off for it. I recapped the flask, not eager to find out what Fynn might say if I came home with tequila breath. I was even less eager to hear one of

Dad's lectures if he ever found out. Partly, I think, because of the grief it's caused Uncle Ed, Dad never touches the stuff.

Once last fall, I'd finished a half-empty beer Uncle Ed had left on my porch—mostly to impress Galen. The end result? Grampa grounded me for a month, and let's just say that Galen had to throw away his shoes and socks.

The Flash repocketed his flask and laughed. "Shooter," he said, "I was thinking it would be amazing to do a feature project on this Native American youth camp. I could do sidebars on Mrs. Wilhelm and the rice harvest. Personality profiles on a couple of the kids. You're not doing anything else, are you?"

Fynn had Natalie. Grampa had Clementine. The house was spotless.

Of course I wasn't doing anything else.

I picked up the Oreo wrapper, dropped it into the trash can, and said, "I'd signed on for a one-day shoot, but . . ."

In just a couple of minutes, my attitude had flip-flopped. I liked hanging out with somebody who wasn't being careful with me. My struggles at the shoot and in the darkroom faded. I told myself I could make Natalie proud and maintain my objectivity.

The Flash and I shook on it. Not spit-shook, just shook.

I hoped I wouldn't live to regret promising a favor to a moderately cute boy wearing a nose ring.

When I got home from the *Examiner*, the blinking red light on the answering machine nagged at me. The message said, "Cassidy Rain, this is Mrs. Owen, Galen's mother. I have a few more questions to ask you about this Native American youth program. I'm sure you've learned more about it since we last spoke. Please return this call as soon as possible."

"Galen's mother," she'd said. Like I could forget.

I erased the message without picking up the phone.

After the evening news, I wandered back into the kitchen and noticed a postcard from Grampa on the table. UNLUCKY IN LAS VEGAS headlined a picture of a cracked slot machine. The other side read:

Dear Rainbow,

Never met a woman so stubborn as that Clementine. She won't so much as let me pick up the check at dinner. All that sass, no wonder she's been married six times. Probably jabbered her husbands to death. I've had enough.

Going back downstairs for more Jell-O.

XOXO, Grampa

P.S. Lost the $300 I'd won on the slots.

Natalie strolled past my open door, carrying four rolls of wallpaper. One had unfurled, and it trailed her like a bridal train.

We do not have a wallpaper kind of house. We have a house with antique white walls and stenciled borders—roosters in the kitchen, cherubs in the bath, pineapples in the dining nook, ivy in the family room and hallway.

Turning into my parents' bedroom, I bumped into Natalie coming back out. She had apparently dropped off her supplies and was hauling out a load of clothes. As we collided, she dropped an armful of jeans, sweatshirts, and sweaters.

"You're exactly what I need," Natalie told me. "Another set of hands. Fynn's been holed up in his Domain all night."

Natalie gathered up most of the pile, carried it back into the master bedroom, and tossed it onto the bed. I picked up a long denim skirt off the hardwood floor and followed her in. I realized then that the skirt in my hand, the clothes she'd been carrying out—they'd belonged to my mother. I couldn't understand why Natalie had even been touching Mom's clothes.

Glancing around the master bedroom, I couldn't believe what Natalie had done, either. Mom's ballerina jewelry box wasn't sitting on the dresser. Her collection of antique hats, from pillbox to cowpoke, had been stripped from the brass rack.

Her traditional tear dress was gone.

Natalie tugged a BEAK 'EM, HAWKS sweatshirt onto its plastic hanger and hung it on the molding of Dad's well-stocked rifle cabinet. She touched the glass doors and then drew back. "Do you think your dad would mind if we move this thing into the basement?" she asked, glancing at me. "Rain?"

I stood in the middle of the room, still holding the denim skirt. Chewie lay in the doorway, nose on his front paws. The spinning ceiling fan offered little relief from the rising humidity.

"Fynn didn't tell you," Natalie said. She sank to the edge of the bed and fiddled with her earring. "When I talked to your dad the other day," she explained, "he—we decided to convert the back porch into a room for him so Fynn and I could move in here."

"What's wrong with Fynn's room?" I asked. "You guys have seemed happy enough sleeping there since your fourth date."

It had just slipped out. That happens sometimes. My mouth malfunctions.

I wiped the sweat from the back of my neck. The previous month, Fynn had ripped out the window-unit air conditioner from the master bedroom and hooked it up in his Domain to cool down his precious computer equipment. Never mind the discomfort to us humans or the dog.

"You need to talk to your brother," Natalie whispered.

What does that mean? I wondered, staring at her worn face. She seemed so tired lately, so different, down to her meatier diet. The heat seemed to be getting to her, even more than to me.

Suddenly, it all made sense. Natalie's shadowed eyes, the all-new, pressed, and buttoned-down Fynn. Their short, stressful engagement. Fynn and Natalie were moving into my parents' room so Fynn's could become a nursery for their baby. Natalie was pregnant and had been for some time.

Fynn should've told me. I was family.

Besides, Natalie would need me, and not just for diapering. I'd grown up in Hannesburg, and I knew people already had to be talking about her being some spoiled Johnson County girl. And never mind that a quarter or so of the women in town were single mothers. In Hannesburg, Natalie was still considered an outsider. And Fynn was a hometown boy, one of the few with a future who hadn't moved away. Lorelei in particular would be sure to broadcast her feelings on the subject.

I blew out a long breath and told Natalie, "No, my brother needs to talk to me."

✲ Laura Ashley's Prissy Twin

FROM MY JOURNAL:

"What are the goals of the program?" the Flash asked Aunt Georgia.

"To give these kids a chance to get together, learn a thing or two, build a bridge. Maybe we'll catch a movie." She chuckled. "Oh, and to have fun. Eat up my cooking."

They'd pulled up a couple of chairs at the foot of the stage. I couldn't help overhearing from behind the curtains as I changed my film.

"What are the challenges?" he asked Aunt Georgia.

"Right now, we're looking at only a few days and a pretty diverse group," she replied. "I've never put together anything like this before. Maybe I should be doing it differently somehow. But mostly, I just think these kids need one another."

I wasn't sure what Aunt Georgia meant, and she didn't explain.

JUNE 30

The museum was Hannesburg's original city hall, built with the town in the early 1900s. Though the sign outside read PRESERVING THE PAST FOR THE FUTURE, the building served more often as a spot for weddings and baby showers. But I'd always liked its feeling of history. The two-story ceiling. The heavy red curtain bordering the stage. Even the cheap but cheerful kitchenette.

Aunt Georgia had brought in oversized pillows and plopped them on the stage like splotches of paint. Marie chose a navy pillow between Dmitri's lime and Spence's burgundy. Queenie picked the yellow one on the other side of Spence. They slipped into their journals, while I skimmed the circle, shooting, staying in the shadows, and the Flash read Aunt Georgia's copy of the *Oklahoma Indian Times*.

Later, Aunt Georgia reached into her backpack. She took out two two-pound boxes of spaghetti, a one-pound plastic bag of rubber bands, two wooden rulers, and a bottle of glue. It made an odd pile on the stage floor.

"I've been thinking," Aunt Georgia said. "You kids could build a bridge." A pasta bridge, from the looks of things. "Say twenty-four inches long," she added, "weighing no more than a pound. We'll see how strong you can make it."

Queenie twisted the orange glue cap. "You heard her," she said. "Think *strong.*"

Spence and Marie reached for the rulers. Dmitri started sketching in his journal, working in suggestions from the group. The Flash followed Aunt Georgia to the kitchenette, and I trailed after them in case she needed help with lunch.

"When you first thought of the road trip," the Flash began, "did you think it would be a way for these teenagers to maintain ties to their heritage?"

That's what Natalie calls "feeding a line." Instead of quoting the source directly, the reporter writes something like "Wilhelm said the road trip would be an opportunity for the American Indian teenagers to maintain ties to their cultural heritage."

Aunt Georgia chuckled. "The first thing I thought was, Ten days with my husband, a handful of teenagers, and a rental minivan? I've gone plumb loco."

The Flash dutifully recorded the quote and then kept his pen poised. His eyes were pure puppy dog, begging the way Chewie's did for Chinese takeout.

"All right," Aunt Georgia said. "I know you're here to do a job." She paused a moment before continuing. "First off, it's the cultural heritage of only two of the kids, and they know a whole heap more about it than I'd have any right to. But this camp is a good deal about science, and agriculture is sure enough a science. That may not be how your people back in St. Louis think of it. But if you ask around here, folks'll tell you that's how it is." She seemed to anticipate his next question. "That's not all it is with the wild-rice harvest, but you'll have to call Dmitri and Marie's mama to see if she'll tell you more. It's not up to me."

I could guess that the harvest was part of Ojibway traditional life—past, present, and future. That being the case, it most likely had some spiritual importance. Aunt Georgia was hinting to the Flash that it might be best for an outsider to leave the details alone. I wasn't sure if he understood her or not.

The Flash seemed about to ask another question. He

opened his mouth and then closed it again, apparently undecided. Then he read back over his quotes.

Aunt Georgia punched the play button on her boom box, and Elvis warned us to stay off of his blue suede shoes. "Young man," she added, popping a bowl into the microwave, "I hope you can stomach my cooking."

"Thanks," the Flash answered, "but I can't accept anything from a source."

"You what?" I asked, shocked at his manners.

"It's a rule," he informed me, sticking his pen behind his ear. "If you don't believe me, Shooter, you're free to ask Nat."

Six minutes later, the microwave beeped, and Aunt Georgia lifted the lid off of the bowl, releasing the smell of homemade chicken noodle soup. I lined up with Spence and Queenie for lunch.

"Maybe I should call Nat," the Flash said, "just in case."

Queenie nodded at the entryway. "Pay phone's in the foyer," she said.

"No time like the Pez-ent," Spence agreed as Dmitri and Marie walked over.

"Is he always like that?" Dmitri asked, his eyes tracking the Flash's departure.

"I don't know," I answered. "We met yesterday."

Taking the hint from Spence, Marie gave us all a Pez candy from a Tweety dispenser. "I like his coat," she said.

After Aunt Georgia served up our bowls, I took a seat on the stage between the Headbirds. Queenie had run out with Spence to fetch the cooler of Cokes from the back of Aunt Georgia's station wagon.

As I was raising my first spoonful of broth, the Flash returned and announced, "Nat says that as long as it's edible, drinkable, or under five bucks, I'm good to go."

He'd been commuting to Hannesburg every day from his frat house in Lawrence. He'd already mentioned twice that the house mom had summers off. I suspected it'd been a while since his last home-cooked meal.

When I arrived home, the message light was blinking.

The caller said, "Cassidy Rain, this is Mrs. Owen again. Please give me a call. I must prepare to counter Mrs. Wilhelm's proposed city expenditure, and I can't very well discuss it with *her,* now can I?"

Somebody needed to tell Mrs. Owen that stalking was illegal.

No doubt she'd heard by now that I was covering Indian Camp for the paper, and she'd known all along that I'd have inside information. But I had no intention of sitting down and giving her the ammo she needed to defeat Aunt Georgia.

I hit the button to erase.

The next time the phone rang, it was Dad, who said, "It's a beautiful eighty degrees today here at Andersen Air Force Base." He congratulated me on my photo gig with the *Examiner* and made me promise to send him the clips.

I brought up Natalie only once, just long enough to give her credit for letting me shoot the story.

Dad brought up Fynn only once, just long enough to mention how my brother had wanted me to join Indian

Camp. "You're the smart one," Dad concluded. "Photography is your future. Don't let what anybody says convince you otherwise. A person shouldn't let her heritage hold her back."

I didn't say anything, just held tightly to the phone and listened as he kept lecturing. I couldn't even come up with an "I love you, too" when we traded good-byes.

After hanging up, I sat up on my quilt and looked toward the top shelf of my bookcase, from the photo of Mom flying a long-tailed kite to the one of Dad posed in front of a C-130.

It'd been a long time since Dad and I had shared a "Yes, sir!" kind of moment.

At Indian Camp, the Flash had given me a copy of the Fourth of July tab and told me that Natalie had driven to Kansas City to have high tea and to debate wedding plans with her mother on the Country Club Plaza.

Alice's tea party in Wonderland didn't last as long. At 9:30, Natalie still wasn't back.

In his Domain, Fynn cranked up the volume on a Meat Loaf song. I could hear it through my open window, over the rotating fan that blew across a cookie pan I'd filled with ice water.

I'd been lying on my bedroom carpet in front of the fan, reading. When I finished Natalie's article on local veterans, I remembered my tape recorder. Dad had given it to me the previous Christmas, saying he often missed the sound of my voice. I'd sent one taped letter right away but none since Galen's death.

When I opened my hope chest, I saw Mom's tear dress, folded with even corners beneath the tape recorder, my Bible, my unanswered mail, and an envelope of old photos. Natalie must have placed the dress in there, I realized. She'd had some idea of how much it meant.

Pressing the play button on the recorder, I began: "Hi, Dad. You asked the other day about Natalie. It's nice having another girl in the house. I can talk to her like I would a big sister. She's blond but not Blond, if you know what I mean. . . ."

Natalie's VW converta-Bug chugged into the gravel driveway, and I clicked the stop button.

Fynn's stereo blasted, "I'd Do Anything for Love (But I Won't Do That)." Fynn was working on the promo site for Not Your Wild West Show. He only listens to the vintage *Bat Out of Hell* albums when he's on deadline. And when Fynn's on deadline, it's best to leave him alone. Under the circumstances, Natalie would know better than to venture into his Domain. At least I hoped so.

I found her sitting on the front porch step. The screen door banged behind me, startling Chewie, who sprang from her side into the crabgrass.

Natalie didn't turn, didn't move at all. I moved slowly, shocked by what I saw.

She'd taken out her pirate earring. She'd traded in her T-shirt, overalls, and hiking boots for a white cotton dress, sheer white hose, and black patent flats. Her hair had been curled, like with a curling iron, and I suspected the use of hair spray—*aerosol* hair spray. Natalie looked horrible, absolutely hideous, like Laura Ashley's prissy twin.

As I sat on it, the porch swing creaked. I peeled a bit of paint off of my left thumbnail, hoping the marriage proposal hadn't been panic talking. "Natalie," I said, "I know about the baby."

Her thin shoulders slumped slightly. She turned to look at me, and the bones of her face looked skull-like. Sharp. "Fynn finally told you?" she asked.

"Figured it out myself," I said, not sure it had been my place to bring up the subject. When she didn't answer, I added, "Did you have a good tea?"

Natalie pushed up from the stairs and joined me on the swing. "You've met my mom," she said. "Unwed mothers are one of her pet rants."

Sounded serious. "Did you tell her Fynn is a Republican?" I asked.

"Next time," she said, "I'll lead with it."

As the breeze rattled our wind chime, we swung side by side.

"She just doesn't understand me," Natalie announced. "She wants me to get a PR job like hers in some mauve-colored office at an agency on College Boulevard. Had one all lined up, too, with the wife of one of Dad's golfing buddies from the club. Mom thinks I took the offer at the *Examiner* just to upset her. She thinks I'm just rebelling from subdivision life."

I remembered my one lunch with the Lewises. It was the same week Fynn had gone corporate, and he'd fit right in at the Bennigan's in Overland Park. But before we'd left Hannesburg, Natalie had told him it wasn't necessary to get so dressed up. That day, she'd worn her overalls and okayed my ladybug-patch jeans.

In a conversation mostly made up of criticizing Natalie's outfit, quizzing Fynn about his computer business, and toasting the Lewises' yard for being recognized as "Lawn of the Month," her mother had managed to bring up the phrase "living in sin" twice.

I couldn't help wondering if Mrs. Lewis had been right about Natalie rebelling against the suburbs and whether Natalie's moving in with Fynn had been part of it. I hoped not. "Why didn't anybody tell me?" I asked. "About the baby, I mean."

"Fynn and I fought," she explained, watching Chewie chase the fireflies. "Neither of us wanted to tell anybody about the baby until my second month. If something is going to go wrong with a pregnancy, it usually happens early. But Fynn didn't want to tell you only half the truth, and I wanted to announce the engagement right away."

She seemed so lost, and suddenly, I felt like the older, more mature one. More than anything, I wanted to shield Natalie and my future niece or nephew from any bullet words, no matter if they came from local gossips, mother-daughter tea parties, or my own big brother's Domain. I was going to be an aunt. The baby had become my top priority.

"How was your doctor's appointment?" I asked.

"Eight weeks and counting," Natalie reported.

The wind carried Meat Loaf's "Life Is a Lemon and I Want My Money Back."

TRAILER PARK DREAMS

FROM MY JOURNAL:

The night of the Winter Enchantment Extravaganza, I was the cardboard snowflake who asked the Holiday Queen for permission to touch her braided hair.

"You may," she answered, gracing my shoulder with the crimson star at the end of her plastic glitter wand.

I tugged off one white glove and raised my fingertips to the weave over her ear, careful not to disturb Her Majesty's rhinestone tiara.

It was the first time I'd ever touched a black person's hair. I'd been curious about how the texture might feel under my fingertips.

Nothing less, nothing more.

We were only five.

JULY 1

Queenie walked into the museum and greeted all with "What do you know?"

Marie looked up from her navy pillow and answered, "The name Pez is from the first, middle, and last letters of *pfefferminz*, the German word for 'peppermint.'"

I made a mental note: Marie knew how to speak to people in their own languages, and Queenie had found a new friend. I told myself I didn't care and attached my lens to shoot from the far-right-hand corner of the stage.

During their interview with the Flash, Dmitri and Marie seemed shy. They spoke in soft voices, avoided his eyes, and sat on their pillows at angles away from him. But they still answered about growing up in Minneapolis and on the Leech Lake Reservation. They told him about how their tribe was called the Chippewa and Ojibway and Annishinabe. They spelled the tribal names, and they told him about harvesting wild rice from the rivers and lakes. Their father was a trader and mechanic, Marie said. Their mother would begin classes at Haskell in the fall.

When Aunt Georgia had first mentioned the trip to the Headbirds' reservation, I'd wondered why she had decided on it. But after hearing Dmitri and Marie talk, I realized it wasn't just me who felt like part of her was someplace else. Going home meant something, like with Mom and me heading down to Oklahoma.

I wondered then if Marie and Dmitri weren't exactly shy. Maybe they felt like they shouldn't have to explain themselves. Like they didn't particularly care if Hannesburg got a glimpse into their lives. Aunt Georgia was always polite, but she didn't seem overly thrilled to have the Flash around all the time. Of course when she'd said he could sit in, Aunt Georgia couldn't have known he'd plan to do a whole feature project, instead of just a regular news story. Her understanding had been that he'd be out of the way in an hour or two.

Just then, it was clear that I'd made a mistake by pulling the *Examiner* into Indian Camp. Worse, I was probably the reason Aunt Georgia was putting up with the Flash being there. My fault, not his.

Meanwhile, Queenie and Spence hauled in a foldout table from the storage closet. Then Dmitri and Marie carefully transferred the newspaper-covered cardboard supporting all three parts of the soon-to-be connected pasta bridge from the stage to the table in the center of the museum.

After I'd left the day before, the Indian Campers had apparently morphed into a dedicated pasta construction team. Each brace of the bridge was ten noodles thick, held together with rubber bands and secured with glue in criss-cross patterns. One problem—Marie had poured on the glue, using up a fourth of the bottle.

"You stuck them to the paper," Spence said. He pulled at one of the longer side supports, and the end of a noodle snapped off.

"Sorry," Marie replied.

As I pulled my camera's focus from Marie's face, Aunt Georgia fiddled with her boom box and Elvis began singing about ghetto life. When Aunt Georgia returned to the kitchenette to resume making fried bologna sandwiches, I shot a photo of her instead.

"Slow and easy," Dmitri answered, carefully tearing the bridge segments free, ignoring bits of paper still stuck to them.

I returned my focus to the Headbirds. Fynn and I used to be like Dmitri and Marie, fixing each other's problems, or trying to anyway. I let go of a long breath, promising myself to help Fynn with Natalie and the baby. I decided to follow Dmitri's example and take it slow.

"Pasta," Queenie announced, "comes from golden wheat." Her Majesty picked up one of the spaghetti boxes and added, "The word *pasta* means 'paste' or 'dough.'"

I hoped she wasn't in a cooking phase. We'd never hear the end of it.

While the Indian Campers worked, I moved to sit on the edge of the stage, swinging my legs, sucking a piece of candy from Marie's Dino dispenser. My mind was still on Natalie. I decided to stop by the sale at Lydia's Rethreads and pick up a baby jumper, maybe one that said FUTURE PRESIDENT, or FUTURE JAYHAWK, or GIMME MILK!

In typical Queenie fashion, she ruined my plan by asking Marie whether she wanted to go to Lydia's later on. I swallowed hard, trying not to give in to disappointment. But things were awkward enough as it was, and Queenie would ask too many questions if I bought a baby gift in front of her.

Marie lifted the base of the bridge and replied, "Okay. How about you, Rain?"

I didn't have to glance at Queenie's expression to know she hadn't meant to include me.

To hide my face, I looked through the viewfinder. "Got plans," I said, "but thanks."

I was grateful that the pasta bridge construction had reached a critical stage, commanding everybody's attention. As Marie and Dmitri held the base of the bridge in place, Spence squeezed glue onto the points where it was supposed to attach to the sides. It was a struggle. Each time the Headbirds loosened their hold, the whole structure teetered. If they'd let go, it would've been sure to topple.

"It's not working," Dmitri said.

I knew Aunt Georgia was listening. But she stayed put, continuing with lunch preparations, apparently deciding this final phase of construction would have to succeed or fail without her input.

As Spence let slip a word not fit for grown-up ears, I began to worry about how the campers might come across in the Flash's article. Failure seemed likely.

Just when it looked like the Indian Campers were going to give up, Queenie grabbed the spaghetti boxes and placed one on each side of the bridge, bracing it so the glue could dry overnight. It was, of course, the perfect thing to do.

Spence grinned and announced, "It's a go!"

As the Indian Campers surveyed their masterpiece, the Flash reknotted the belt on his trench coat and approached Queenie.

"Write this down," she said. "Some people say that pasta was invented thousands of years ago in China, but nobody knows for sure."

The Flash dutifully scribbled something before asking, "What brings you here?"

Queenie squared her shoulders and asked, "Don't you mean 'Why is an African-American girl at a Native American program?'"

"Sure," the Flash answered, pen perched, "that's exactly what I meant."

The Headbirds and Spence moved to stand by me against the stage.

"Uh-oh," Spence whispered, accepting candy from Marie.

Queenie spoke clearly, like she wanted to make sure the Flash didn't misquote her—like she'd have a lot to say about it if he did. "My aunt Suzanne has been tracing our family tree for the reunion next month at her place in Miami," she explained, "and, come to find out, one of my great-grandfathers was a Native American."

The word *cousin* sneaked onto my tongue, and I didn't like the way it tasted. As if stealing Galen hadn't been enough, now Queenie was barging in on my cultural territory. Granted, she was no guru-seeking, crystal-waving, long-lost descendant of an Indian "princess," but still . . . knowing Queenie, genealogy was her phase of the week.

"What tribe, Nation, or band?" the Flash asked, obviously impressed with his growing grip on the terminology.

"I expect," Queenie said, "Aunt Suzanne will get back to me on that."

Dmitri followed Aunt Georgia out of the museum, carrying the leftover potato salad to her station wagon. Unlike Spence, who was being interviewed by the Flash, I didn't feel the need to sneak looks at Marie and Queenie.

Of course, no boys sneak looks at me anymore, I thought, and then shoved the idea away as petty. What kind of person was I turning into?

It was past time for me to leave.

Remembering Mr. Headbird was a trader, I rushed out of the museum after Dmitri and called, "Wait up!"

On the way to Blue Heaven Trailer Park, Dmitri and I

talked about Jayhawks basketball and why I thought his family needed at least a storm cellar to live safely in Kansas during tornado season. The words stumbled, not sure where to go next.

When Dmitri left me standing alone in front of his new trailer, I took my first close look at Blue Heaven. Cement porches hosted petunia pots, barbecue grills, and lawn furniture. Sunburned, half-naked little kids played with matches and ash snakes on gravel drive-throughs. I held on tight to my camera and my two crisp twenty-dollar bills, fresh from the cash machine. I wasn't the kind of girl who hung out at the trailer park.

I didn't want a reputation like Lorelei's.

"This looks like what you want," Dmitri said, jumping down from his doorway, holding a dreamcatcher. "Hang it above the bed."

"It's beautiful," I said, "but dreamcatchers are kind of . . . trendy, don't you think?"

"My mother made it," he answered.

What with that foot crowding my mouth, I could hardly find a reply. Too bad Dmitri couldn't sell me a word-catcher to let good ones through and trap the rest.

It was just that I'd seen so many tacky-looking dreamcatchers over the years, the kind with fakelore gift tags and flamingo-pink feathers. I looked again, more closely this time. The one Dmitri had shown me was beautiful. Being the real thing made a huge difference.

Dmitri gestured to the doorway. "Want to come in and think it over?" he asked.

So I did. I'd thought the trailer would be like a camper, long and narrow, no privacy. I hadn't expected three bedrooms. It was more like a house. Some of the spaces were tight, though. Dmitri's family might be able to squeeze around the kitchen table, but then nobody could open the fridge.

Butterfly magnets held cards to the fridge door, and each card featured a design in black ink. Depending on how I looked at them, the pictures showed something different. It was a kind of illusion, created by overlapping images, overlapping lines. In my favorite, the hole in an oak was the eye of an elder or, from a different angle, of a raven. The oak's roots gathered into the grandmother's hand or, depending again on the angle, into talons curled around a turtle.

Then I spotted another card, half-hidden behind a list of groceries. The design on that one was of a boy who looked a lot like Dmitri—glasses, blue jeans, and all—flying a long-tailed kite. I changed my mind. The kite flier became my favorite.

Dmitri handed me a Dixie cup of ice water, explaining, "I draw the designs, and Dad sells the cards at powwows. We put that one on T-shirts."

The waxy cup chilled my fingers. "You're kidding," I said. "You drew those?" Realizing how I'd sounded, I added, "They're beautiful." What was with me? *Beautiful* was every fourth word out of my mouth.

Dmitri hung the dreamcatcher on a plastic hook above a box of art supplies.

"I'm looking for a gift for Fynn's fiancée," I explained,

trying to save the moment.

Dmitri took off his glasses, polishing them with the tail of his Minnesota Twins T-shirt. "The white girl?" he asked.

"Natalie," I said.

"My brother met a Kiowa girl from Lawrence," Dmitri told me. "Ron has been seeing her for about a month."

Either Dmitri was telling me that he didn't approve of Fynn's choice or just that he himself had a preference for Indian girls. Other than his sister and—if I wanted to be generous—Queenie, the only local Indian girl near his age happened to be me. My camera strap felt heavy on my shoulder. "I have to go to the bathroom," I said.

He nodded toward the back of the trailer.

It wasn't like I could get lost. The tiny bathroom was sparse—no medicine cabinet, no mirror, no towel racks. The Headbirds were lucky to have the tub and shower-head. I washed my hands and considered mentioning to Dmitri something we had in common, our Ojibway heritage. But I'd grown up so far away from it. I felt ashamed by how much I didn't know.

Mom had always tried to tell Dad that Fynn and I needed to know about our entire family heritage. Dad would always reply that there was a lot he didn't know himself, and it sure hadn't hurt him. We were only St. Patty's Day Irish and Bierfest German, but I was pretty sure they hadn't been talking about those particular family lines.

On the way back to Dmitri, I peeked through one of the cracked-open bedroom doors at a collector's display of Pez dispensers. Marie's, no doubt. Bullwinkle, Mowgli,

Baloo, Tinkerbell, a witch, a pirate, a skull, Mary Poppins, Uncle Sam, Tweety, Winnie-the-Pooh, Batgirl, Joker, Garfield, Snoopy, Gonzo, Pebbles, Dino, and many, many more, some in multiple copies, with handles of different colors.

A couple of T-shirts littered the bed. A stack of *Teen Lifestyles* magazines had tipped over on the floor. The only thing in perfect order was her Pez collection.

The sign of a healthy mind, I thought.

When I returned to the kitchen area, I had a question ready. "Marie and Pez," I said. "What's the deal?"

Dmitri took a sip from his Dixie cup. "Two summers ago, she got mono and had to stay home with my mother. So Ron and I sent her Pez dispensers from the road."

It wasn't photography, but then, collecting Pez probably didn't deplete her budget. "Do you like it here?" I asked Dmitri. "In Hannesburg?"

"My parents were talking about getting a place in Lawrence," he answered, "but it's a lot more expensive. So we're saving up for a house here."

That didn't exactly answer my question, but I didn't want to prod.

Then before I could think of a new topic, Dmitri went on: "I don't know. I'm not trying to come down on your hometown or anything, but . . . Well, everybody here knows one another. And I'm . . ."

My whole life, I'd known everyone in town, and that's exactly what I didn't like about it. Through the open windows, I heard little kids screeching, laughing, playing with fireworks. I briefly thought of Galen, and suddenly it seemed disloyal to be there all alone with Dmitri. I wondered, too, if anyone had seen me come in to the trailer and what they might say. It wasn't like Marie or his mother was home. I glanced at the door but then realized Dmitri was probably waiting for me to reply.

"You're fine," I announced. As soon as the word left my lips, I cringed. "I don't mean fine like, you know, *fine,* good-looking—not that you're bad-looking." It was just getting worse. "I just meant that you're okay—not that you're *just* okay." Shut up, shut up, shut up, shut up, I thought. "I mean you're—"

"Fine," Dmitri said, finishing my sentence. "Don't worry, I know what you mean."

Nothing seemed to be going my way. I still wanted to get a snap-up jumper from Lydia's Rethreads, not a dreamcatcher. But then I thought about it. Queenie always had to try on every single thing in the shop before making up her mind. She and Marie would probably be at Lydia's for a couple of hours at least. On the one hand, I wasn't in the mood to deal with Her Majesty. On the other hand, somehow I knew it was important to reach out to Natalie right away.

I shifted my weight from one foot to the other, undecided.

"I'll take the dreamcatcher," I announced a moment later, handing Dmitri my cash. Time was short, choices were limited, and it did make a certain amount of sense. After all, when babies aren't eating or hollering or pooping, they're usually asleep.

With professional flair, Dmitri presented me with my

change, tissue-wrapped the dreamcatcher, bagged it, and gave me a handwritten receipt. He pushed up his Clark Kent glasses and said, "Thank you, ma'am."

Still clutching the paper bag Dmitri had given me, I passed the Trail of Tears painting that Mom had long ago hung in our hallway and tracked down Natalie in what used to be Fynn's room. She was replacing his navy curtains with a sunflower-print set.

From the top rung of the three-step ladder, she said, "Maybe I'm getting ahead of myself, but I wanted to do something. . . ."

The way I had it figured, the baby would sleep in their room, but maybe decorating was a mommy thing, like a mother bird softening her nest.

"Where's Fynn?" I asked.

"Running," Natalie said, climbing down to show me a scuffed green rocking chair I'd never seen before. "Eight bucks at a garage sale," she announced. "I don't know, though. It needs something."

I wondered where she'd taken Fynn's dresser and whether a pregnant woman should've been moving furniture and climbing ladders, especially one who had a fiancé to lend her a hand.

"Maybe I'll just have Fynn paint it," Natalie said, looking at me. "You okay with all this, the house being turned upside down, your becoming an aunt?"

"If I can dust, I can diaper," I assured her, offering the bag. "For the baby," I said.

She moved to Fynn's twin bed, took the gift, and

exclaimed, "Aiyana's first gift!"

"Aiyana?" I asked.

Natalie held up the dreamcatcher, and its web snared the window light. "I just know the baby is a girl," she answered. "A mother can sense these things."

Aiyana is an old name, a musical name. My mom's name, after her Cherokee great-grandmother. It means "forever flowering."

I smiled at Natalie and noticed she looked flushed. "Feeling all right?" I asked.

She set her palm on her belly and explained, "What they don't tell you about morning sickness is that it can last all day."

Stop the Presses

FROM MY JOURNAL:

With a best friend, there's a commitment. A second-best friend is trickier. A second-best friend knows you and most of your secrets, and you know her and most of hers. And, knowing all of that, both of you decide the friendship is only second-best.

Nobody's more dangerous than an ex-second-best friend.

JULY 2

On Sunday, Indian Camp started at one o'clock, giving Spence and Aunt Georgia time to attend Mass, and giving Queenie time to sing "Morning Has Broken" at First Baptist. As usual since New Year's, I slept in.

The Flash and I cheered when the Indian Campers' pasta bridge proved itself strong enough to support eight pounds. Then I tucked my journal into the stage curtain, moved to the main level, and focused on Dmitri attaching a tiny Chinese umbrella on a toothpick to the top of the bridge. The lines of the bridge framed his face, giving my shot texture.

Behind me, Elvis sang on Aunt Georgia's boom box.

Spence shucked off his Nikes, slid across the stage in his socks, and did a brief imitation of the King. Marie and Queenie laughed as he rumbled, "Thank you, thank you very much."

As Aunt Georgia retrieved her weights from the top of the bridge, she said, "This puts me in mind of the one in *The Bridge on the River Kwai*."

That was definitely a reference to one of my areas of expertise. Galen and I had seen practically every movie at Mercury Videos, including the award winners. I lowered my camera and added, "Starring Sir Alec Guinness, better known as the senior Obi-Wan."

Resting on my knees, I took a shot of the length of the base. Aunt Georgia had been generous. The construction effort wasn't quite Kwai quality. Bits of newspaper still clung to the glue. The sides were uneven, and the supports had been spaced out, instead of gathered in clusters as on the bridge in the film. If it had been life-sized, a person could've fallen right through the gaps. Or maybe even something bigger could've fallen through, like Natalie's converta-Bug.

"What an accomplishment," Spence said, jumping down from the stage and stepping into my frame. "Rain, you're missing out."

"Don't be presumptuous," I answered, using my old spelling word.

"Don't you mean Pez-umptuous?" he asked, munching a candy.

If I'd been a spelling bee, I would've stung him.

Instead, I took another shot, this one of Aunt Georgia and the Indian Campers with the bridge, Spence and the

Headbirds on one side, Aunt Georgia and Queenie on the other. Natalie would never run it—too posed—but I could hand out a few prints as souvenirs. I'd already promised to make everybody copies of the best pictures.

Once the initial excitement began to dim, Aunt Georgia headed to the door to pick up take-out lunches and cake from the coffee shop. She said, "After we eat, let's try eight and a quarter. We'll keep going on up and see how much she holds."

I knew why she was serving lunch first. Sooner or later, as the weights became heavier, the bridge would break. Before that happened, Aunt Georgia wanted to give everyone a chance to celebrate.

Once she'd left, the Flash circled the Indian Campers at the table, readied his pen, and asked, "Any opinions on the petition Mrs. Owen has been circulating?"

What petition? I thought.

The Flash paged through his notes and added, "It's to—and I quote—'let the city council know the citizens have had it with the mayor's pet projects and that we're not going to 'let him throw money away'"—he glanced up—"'on this program.'"

Mrs. Owen's letter had been just one person's opinion, but a petition . . .

"What an atrocity of discriminatory injustice!" Spence proclaimed.

"We'll write our own letter to the editor," Queenie said. She ran to the stage to get her journal and then repeated, "A-tro-ci-ty of dis-crim-in-a-tor-y in-jus-tice," obviously writing down the phrase as she returned to the group.

"Where did you get that?" Marie asked Spence.

"His parents are lawyers," Dmitri reminded her.

"Are you suing the city?" the Flash asked, like he was hoping for a juicier clip.

My mind filled with visions of lawsuit headlines, letters to the editor, and coffee-shop jokes about the natives getting restless. I hiked up the camera strap on my shoulder and asked, "What do you all think you're doing?"

The Flash replied, "They're writing a letter to the editor to rebut Mrs. Owen's petition challenging the proposed city financing of this Native American youth program."

That sounded too much like he'd already drafted his lead.

"The city council meets on Monday," I said, relieved at the obvious excuse to block their plan. "The *Examiner* comes out on Wednesday. There's no way your letter could be published before the vote, so why bother?"

Still clutching her journal, Queenie held up a finger for each option and said, "We could make copies of our letter and stick them under windshield wipers, or start our own petition, or we could sue, or . . . we could just talk to Mrs. Owen. She was my fifth-grade homeroom mother, and I think—"

"How about letting it go?" I asked, adjusting my camera strap.

For Mrs. Owen, this was about politics. It was the kind of thing nobody bothered to read about in the local paper. For me, it was about Galen. I didn't want any more trouble with his mother, and I didn't want Queenie in his house.

Besides, I'd grown up in Hannesburg, and Queenie was forgetting that—short of Mrs. Owen backing off—nothing could push our city council members one way or the other. They were all newly reelected, and the next race was too far away.

"It's not that big of a deal," I added, taking a step to face Her Majesty, each of us on opposite sides of the pasta bridge. I hadn't spoken directly to Queenie like that since tossing her out of what had been our locker.

"It's about *us*," she answered. "You're here for the paper, not Indian Camp."

Queenie had a point. A tiny, glowing point. A flicker on a long-fused package of dynamite that had been burning since the day I'd first found out about her and Galen.

"See you at the newsroom," I told the Flash, backing off, positive that nobody else needed to get stuck in the middle of my ongoing feud with Her Majesty.

In another life, maybe the Indian Campers themselves would've figured out what to do about the petition, or maybe they would've even decided it wasn't worth their trouble. I could've come back the next day, ridden out the job, and returned to my hermit habits. But it wasn't another life.

When I turned fast to leave, my camera strap swung, gaining momentum, launching my Nikon into the pasta bridge. I tried to catch them both—the bridge and my camera—but no.

They fell, crashing, smashing, my camera smacking and clunking, the glued pasta exploding, shattering on the tile floor, and as I fought for balance, the sole of my right boot landed on the center of the bridge, breaking it into five skittering pieces. A few spaghetti noodles split off and shot across the room.

An accident, I swear.

Marie and Dmitri stepped back. Spence and the Flash whispered, "Ouch."

Queenie picked up a hunk of pasta, looked at me, and said, "You are so dead."

I didn't answer. I didn't know what to say.

As Dmitri, Marie, and Spence slowly began to gather up what was left of the bridge, I picked up my broken camera. On the main floor of the museum, the quiet boiled, simmered, and finally stilled.

Marie looked up at me, her hands full of pasta. "Rain," she said, "you know this Mrs. Owen, right? Why don't you try to change her mind?"

It was an all-but-gift-wrapped chance to make everything better. Of course Marie couldn't realize what she'd asked of me. No matter what she might have heard since moving to Hannesburg, she couldn't guess at the full history between Galen's mom and me.

I took a breath and promised to try, briefly wondering if I'd ever be able to find the words to convince Mrs. Owen and whether Natalie would really fire me for getting involved, for the conflict of interest.

A minute or so later, I pushed out of the front doors of the museum and realized Queenie was only steps behind me.

"What?" I asked, turning to face her.

"What, yourself," she replied. "Since when are you

worried about Mrs. Owen? She sure didn't seem to miss you at Galen's funeral."

My eyes fell to the red peonies bordering the brick building, and I could almost see Queenie standing in front of Galen's mourners, beside his coffin, reading some pretty words she'd scribbled in a poetry phase.

"I heard you were the star," I answered, taking a step toward her.

"Galen was my boyfriend until you stole him," she said, holding her ground.

I couldn't believe she was playing the victim. "I know you dumped him for Ernie on the day of the dance," I declared. "Galen told me so himself."

"For your information," Queenie answered, "Ernie is my friend. The fact is that Galen told me he was going over to *your* house that night, instead of taking me to the party. What was I supposed to do? Stay home by myself? And how dare you act so innocent? Everybody knows it was you who was with Galen on the night he died. That's why Mrs. Owen ordered you to sit out his funeral. That's why when she decided one of his friends should stand up and say something, she called me. That's why—"

I left Queenie in midrant and took off for the death place.

My toes throbbed and my shins ached from running almost four miles in cowboy boots. My side hurt from where my battered camera had banged against it. My sweaty fingers closed around the hot iron, and my palms burned.

It was a black wrought-iron gate, and it towered over

me. It was a peacocky gate, fussy and proud. It was the gate to the Garden of Roses Cemetery, and Galen's grave waited on the other side. I hadn't been there, not once, not even to pay respects to my own mom, since finding out that Galen had died.

I tightened my grip, trying to figure out what had happened between him and Queenie. All I knew for sure was that he'd shown up on my front porch with that empty look on his face, and she'd gone to the dance with Ernie. I couldn't help wondering whether Galen had died without telling me the whole truth, and I couldn't help wondering why he would've lied. It was tempting to think that maybe he'd just wanted to spend time with me that night.

I let go of the gate, reached down, and snapped off a spray of Queen Anne's lace, desperate to touch something pretty. Not even caring that it would kill the bloom.

From where I was standing, I couldn't see Galen's grave, but it wasn't hard to imagine what it looked like.

On Memorial Day, Fynn had told me the stone was gray and flat, placed beneath a sugar maple. It listed his full name, Galen Hannes Owen, with his birth date and death date, followed by LOVING SON.

A mosquito landed on my right hand. I smacked it, wiped its bloody guts on the gate, and walked away, holding my weed flower. My camera strap rubbed my shoulder, and my steps fell lopsided. It was as close as I had come to what everyone said was the right ritual, the right thing to do, but it didn't feel right to me.

A Taste for Green Bean Casserole

FROM MY JOURNAL:

"You can stand anything for three weeks," Galen had claimed.

I'd wanted the money to buy film, and minimum wage sounded like a fortune. Grampa saying it was no job for a girl just made me that much more determined.

So at sunrise, a witch named Maggie hauled us and five foulmouthed high-school boys in a pickup bed to the Tischers' cornfield. We all wore jeans and flannel shirts to protect us from the sharp leaves, and caps to shield us from the July sunshine.

Corn rows stretched a mile long. Galen and I walked fast, yanking tassels from the top of five-foot cornstalks. I didn't mind the field mice or the snakes, not like the mosquitoes crawling beneath my clothes. In the morning, mud coated my sneakers, and then as the sun rose, sweat poured across my aching back, arms, and shoulders. After work, we checked our hair for ticks, and Fynn had to burn one off of my head.

JULY 2

At sunset, I sat on a stump in Aunt Georgia's garden. She handed me a plate of two cold barbecued chicken legs and microwaved corn on the cob. Her parrot, Elvis, hopped from Aunt Georgia's shoulder onto the statue of a man, which was surrounded by peach rosebushes.

The marker read: SAINT FIACRE, PATRON SAINT OF TAXI DRIVERS AND GARDENERS.

While I polished off dinner, Aunt Georgia weeded her radishes, studied her broccoli, and checked the ripeness of her corn.

"Sorry I messed up Indian Camp," I called.

"Hush," Aunt Georgia answered. "Let yourself be, hon. Just let yourself be." She moved to the statue, and Elvis hopped back onto her shoulder.

I touched the Queen Anne's lace that I'd picked at the cemetery. It was sticking out, Hawaiian-style, from behind my ear.

Near as I could tell, Spence had gone out for the night, probably with Her Majesty and the gang. Finding him not there had been a relief.

"Doesn't matter," I whispered, glancing at Aunt Georgia's tomato-red hair. I still wasn't used to the new hue. It looked too out of place.

Don't get me wrong. I've seen a couple of mixed-blood people with naturally red hair. Aunt Georgia's new look didn't fall into that category, though.

I caught myself staring and looked down at my chicken bones instead.

"Like my dye job?" Aunt Georgia asked, taking a seat on the small concrete bench beside me. "Bernadette Rae charged me forty bucks."

It seemed best to keep my opinion to myself. I didn't want to hurt her feelings.

Instead, I thought about Aunt Georgia and hair, Indian Campers and pasta bridges, the city council and conflicts of interest, the coming baby and the rice harvest, and finally about Mrs. Owen and Galen's birthday—only two days away.

"Galen's birthday is coming up," I said.

It seemed safe to talk to Aunt Georgia about it. She was the person I felt most comfortable asking for advice, especially with Grampa gone and Fynn so preoccupied. But I still felt a slight tremor run through my body, and so I took a moment to calm myself. The last thing I wanted to do was to break down again. There'd been too many days when all I did was cry. I tried hard to focus.

Aunt Georgia's hand wrapped over mine and squeezed briefly. I'd never noticed before how visible her veins had become, how my hand had grown to the same size as hers.

"I know, hon," Aunt Georgia said. "I know."

I set my plate aside. "I promised him—we promised each other to always celebrate each other's birthdays. Even with him gone, I still feel like I should . . . do something."

Aunt Georgia didn't answer, but I knew she understood how I felt about the promise. After all, she was one of the people who'd taught me what a promise meant.

I glanced down at my black fingernails. "What am I going to do?"

Aunt Georgia stayed silent so long, I began to wonder if she'd heard me. Her gaze seemed lost in the orange-and-pink sunset. Then Aunt Georgia wiped the veil of sweat from her forehead and blew out a long, tired breath. "I just don't know," she said slowly. "But you'll find a way. I'm sure of it. I believe in you, hon."

It had been worth a try, and somehow, just hearing her say she believed in me helped. I thanked her for dinner and then we chatted awhile about everything besides Galen and Indian Camp.

"I almost forgot," Aunt Georgia said, reaching into her backpack. She handed me my journal and a pen. "You might be needing these."

Until then, I hadn't even realized I'd forgotten them at the museum.

Aunt Georgia took my empty plate and glass. "I'd best put up my bird. Why don't you sit a spell." She walked back to the house, slid open the door, and called to me, "How 'bout I give myself a curly home perm and sing one of those cheerful tunes from *Annie*?"

I grinned and yelled back, "I'd like that."

After she disappeared inside, I took a long, deep breath and then, licking my lips, tasted a trace of barbecue sauce. The temperature had started to cool.

Before long, my eyes drifted to Saint Fiacre, surrounded by peach roses, my mother's favorites. I popped the cap off of my pen.

FROM MY JOURNAL:

Nobody ever talks about how my mom died. At least not around me. Maybe because it's old news. Everybody knows she was struck by lightning on her way home from Hein's Grocery Barn. She'd been carrying a paper bag filled with three Granny Smith apples, a bottle of cinnamon, a box of cornstarch, and a pack of light cigarettes. She'd been planning to bake a pie.

The funeral wasn't all bad. I wore something not black on purpose. An orange sundress, out of season, too tight. Dad ironed it before Gramma Scott arrived. He must've sprayed on the whole bottle of starch, because the material felt stiff, and the straps bit my shoulders.

Mourners and hangers-on crowded my house. It seemed like a typical get-together—babies fighting over Binky toys, women eating apple cobbler in the kitchen, neighborhood men watching Chiefs football on the family-room TV.

Galen and I crawled through my bedroom window onto the roof. We sat on the shingles, sharing my quilt. He tried to hold my hand, but I pulled it away, across the shingles, and three or four splinters burned inside my skin.

"I hate football," I said.

"Me, too," Galen answered.

That was the first time I let myself cry.

Maybe an hour later, Mrs. Owen stuck her head out the window, and called, "Come on back in here before you catch your death."

As Galen and I crawled through my window, Mrs. Owen tossed a kitchen towel over my hope chest and set down a glass bowl of her French green bean casserole. She shoveled heaping spoonfuls onto paper plates, handed Galen and me plastic soup spoons, and crossed her arms, waiting.

I didn't want her staring at my stiff orange sundress. I didn't want her in my bedroom, and I didn't want her stupid casserole. The gray soup was mushroom-lumpy, filled with what looked like skinny green worms. I scooped a piece of the torn toast that she'd sprinkled across the top and shoveled it into my mouth. I felt my jawbone chewing and the heaviness as I swallowed and the food went down my throat.

"Eat what you want," Mrs. Owen said, leaving my bedroom door cracked open behind her. "Bring the leftovers back to the buffet table."

I wrinkled my nose and tried another spoonful. This time was different. This time, the casserole tasted warm and familiar and salty and safe. I took bite after bite after bite, and so did Galen. Before long, we'd scraped the whole bowl clean.

⁂ Did Somebody Say "Clueless"?

FROM MY JOURNAL:

For hours, Fynn and I had sat together at the kitchen table, working on his college and scholarship applications. He wrote while I stapled and stacked. At age ten, I was into being a help. We were finishing up when Dad burst into the kitchen.

"Done yet, kids?" he asked, setting a huge pumpkin on the counter.

Fynn handed him whatever essay he'd been working on.

"Reads nice," Dad said a few minutes later, "but all this about the family—kind of personal, don't you think?"

I don't know what that draft of Fynn's essay said, whether it was for admissions or for scholarship, or whether Dad had anything to do with it.

But when my big brother checked over his paperwork for college, he changed the marks in all of the boxes from "Native American/American Indian" to "White."

JULY 3

I took Galen's gift out of my hope chest, raised the leather ties, and, for the first time since he'd died, knotted them around my neck. The crescent-shaped pouch of the necklace fell beneath my collarbone, and I could feel the nubby suede against my skin.

My camera rested on my dresser. A few more scratches, but they weren't the problem. The reflex mirror had been jammed in the up position. Near the film-advance lever, the body had been bent. It would take professional repairs to get my camera working again.

Chewie padded after me to the kitchen door, panting softly.

"Sorry," I told him, "I've got to handle this one by myself."

The message light flashed on my answering machine. Without checking it, I left the house and walked toward Galen's street.

The doorbell was only a doorbell. Small, round, puny. Lighted orange from within.

On the front step, I told myself that Mrs. Owen and I would talk about Indian Camp, not Galen. If it was just politics versus kids, I didn't see why she couldn't let Tahiti Rummel win one. The mayoral rematch was almost two years away, and besides, if she totally stopped him from spending money, what was she going to criticize?

Something warm and fuzzy grazed my bare leg. I jolted, scaring Angel, Galen's silver tiger cat. "Hey, girl," I called, but she sprinted across the manicured grass to hide behind one of the concrete pots of red geraniums that lined the sandstone driveway. I watched her go.

"Cassidy Rain?" The voice was low, insistent. Mrs. Owen stood in one of her gray dresses on the other side of the doorway, twisting the fine chain of her antique watch necklace. "You didn't have to come all the way over," she said.

What with all the fuss, the disaster at Indian Camp, and worrying about the baby, I'd completely forgotten about Mrs. Owen's phone messages. She obviously thought I was there because she'd asked to talk to me about Aunt Georgia's program, which was fine, after all, because I'd told myself that was what I was there to do.

I touched my birthday necklace and crossed the threshold into Galen's home. In the living room, sheer drapes filtered sunlight. Silk lilies grew from porcelain vases. Heart-framed pictures of Galen hung like teardrops on the walls.

Mrs. Owen perched on her famed Louis Quatorze sofa and gestured for me to join her. "The city council meets in a few hours," she said. "I'd—"

"I don't want to talk about Indian Camp, at least not yet," I told her, surprising myself. Even my run-on mouth usually knows better than to run over a grown-up.

From the photographs, Galen's eyes seemed to stare at me from all sides. Galen as a baby, as a toddler, as a little kid. The images looked blankly at me. Then I spotted his most recent school photo—Galen at thirteen forever. That did it.

Before I could even think about anything else, I had to talk to Mrs. Owen about him. No matter what I'd told myself on the way over or on the front step, we had to start with Galen. "People are saying you told me I couldn't come to my best friend's funeral."

Mrs. Owen moved from the sofa to sit on the bench of her baby grand piano. She turned on the brass pole lamp behind her, and her blond hair took on a golden hue. "Tell me, Cassidy Rain," she began, "why weren't you there?"

"I couldn't," I answered. "I couldn't make myself."

I didn't know where Queenie had gotten her information. But in all those times Mrs. Owen had phoned my house, she'd never left a message to say I wasn't welcome.

For a long time, I didn't fully understand why I'd stayed home. But now it made sense. I hadn't gone to Galen's funeral because that would've made his death seem real. Final. I hadn't been ready to deal with that. I didn't want the image of him in a coffin to replace the one of him that night, waving good-bye, in the snow.

Mrs. Owen reached for her necklace and began twisting it back and forth, a bit too hard the last time. It broke. "I'm sorry," she said as the thin chain snaked from her neck. For a moment, she looked like a poor orphan, lost in someone else's mansion. And then she once again became granite in tailored gray. "Cassidy Rain," she said, "do you mean to say you went out with my boy that night without something on your mind?"

I hesitated, remembering my itchy lips. Did she know we'd broken her rule?

"My son deserved better than that," she announced. "Galen was an honor-roll student. Polite. He respected his mother.

"After Pastor Robinson's sermon, Bernadette Rae was whispering to anyone who'd listen that she'd seen you and Galen running around, you know, in the middle of the night. It was awful. People were still crying. The pastor's wife warned her to show respect for the dead. Since you hadn't shown up, the story caught on. People are still talking. My son's memory deserves better than that."

Yes, I thought, we went street-prowling. Yes, Galen ran home instead of getting a ride from Fynn. No, we weren't supposed to have been out that night.

That didn't make us terrible people, did it? Considering what happened, why would anyone care if we'd become more than friends? If somebody spotted us running down the street, how could she have even known?

It felt like I was missing something. But I couldn't imagine what had been so scandalous that it distracted Mrs. Owen from her grief.

She must blame me, I thought. Galen and I had been partners in crime that night, but I was the only one who got away. And the way I had it figured, Mrs. Owen was right. I could've done something to prevent Galen's death.

I almost started to apologize. It was something I'd been wanting to do for a long time. But then I thought about how Mrs. Owen had described Galen: an honor-roll student, polite, and, his worst fear, a mama's boy. I remembered his golden eyelashes, his tempting freckles, and our birthday pledge. "About Indian Camp—" I began.

"Cassidy Rain," Mrs. Owen said, standing, "perhaps it's time you ran along."

On her dinner break, Natalie had come home to work on the nursery. She'd turned the green garage-sale rocking chair so the outside of the back faced up, and she'd propped it level with a cardboard box. Natalie was using stickers to decorate. Smiley faces. Peace signs. Sparkly flowers. A Hello Kitty or two.

I leaned against the open doorway and asked, "Why didn't you tell me?"

"Tell you?" Natalie repeated, sitting cross-legged on the floor.

"About the rumors," I answered, glancing at the hanging dreamcatcher, "the ones about Galen and me and the funeral." I knew I didn't have to specify.

"I didn't know what to do"—she wiped sweat from above her lip—"or, for that matter, if you could handle it. Fynn said that at least until you started . . . talking about Galen again . . . that we should try to keep our lives as separate from Mrs. Owen's as possible. I almost didn't run her letter in the paper, but minority education is a hot topic, and ignoring it because of you . . ."

"Would've been a conflict of interest?" I asked. Apparently, the Flash hadn't yet told Natalie about my demolition of the pasta bridge at Indian Camp.

"Kind of," she answered. "Besides—and don't repeat this—Mrs. Owen sends the *Examiner* two or three letters a week, sometimes the only ones I get. This year, she's brought eleven petitions to the city council and called six emergency meetings of the downtown merchants. The woman is on a tear."

"So Bernadette Rae saw us," I began, "running downtown, and she decided we were—what?"

"Everybody knows," Queenie had said. What baffled me was the sizzle to the story, what had made it headline news.

Dragging herself to her feet, Natalie informed me, "That's not all people were saying, but Rain, it's been months now. Nobody . . . nobody with a life cares."

"Queenie does," I said. "Mrs. Owen. Me."

Natalie set aside her box of stickers and said, "Okay. But in case you're wondering, it was Mrs. Burnham who first told me, not like 'wait till you hear this,' just like 'I thought you should know,' and it's not . . . If Mrs. Owen hadn't been such a control freak and Galen hadn't died, nobody would've thought anything about two kids fooling around."

Natalie blushed, shrugged, and it hit me. The gossip wasn't just that we were a couple or that we were out late on the town. She hadn't meant "fooling around" like goofing off. She'd meant "fooling around" like making out, mashing, tonsil hockey, swapping spit.

"Rain," Natalie told me, "they say you had your sweater off."

"Sweater. Off?" I asked, positive I'd heard her correctly.

"Sweater off" is fairly far into that moist, warm place between prude and pregnant. Natalie's pregnancy, for example, would cause a fuss, but that's just because there'd always be those jealous types gunning for an out-of-town girl who "took away" one of our best-looking boys. But for the most part, nobody bothers to chat about single moms over age eighteen. I can point out at least one in almost every family. It's younger girls messing around that really gets tongues wagging.

I could see where some people would especially want to believe that about me.

In my going-into-ninth-grade class, Missy O'Dell is eight months pregnant, and both Julia Mayland and Tammy Jo Steward have baby boys named Dawson.

Of course, they're all Blue Heaven girls. They aren't

from an Old Town family like me. Or Galen. Whether it's fair or not, people expect that kind of behavior from them. And, to make things worse, Mrs. Owen had made a whole lot of "*my* child would *never*" comments around town about Missy, Julia, and Tammy Jo.

A supposed, scandalous sighting of a fourteen-year-old Old Town girl with Mrs. Owen's dead son—that was practically poetry.

Now I knew what had been dished about me under hair dryers at Bernadette's Beauty Salon, whispered about me behind open lockers in the halls of Hannesburg Middle School, and debated about me under the walnut tree beside the parking lot of the First Baptist Church.

The whole time, I'd thought people were saying I was dangerously depressed, maybe self-absorbed, never scintillating. I wondered if this was how it felt to be Lorelei.

Natalie took an unsteady step. "I've heard all kinds of things," she added. "One story goes that the sheriff hauled you both back here and Grampa kicked Galen out."

"Who said?" I asked. "Bernadette Rae?"

"I don't know," Natalie answered, placing her hand on her belly. "People talk."

"Might've been Lorelei," I muttered. "She's been weird around me ever since she and Fynn broke up."

"Fynn?" Natalie repeated, shuffling out to the bathroom. "My Fynn took a ride on the Lorelei Express?" She sounded more tired than shocked.

I figured the morning sickness had returned.

A couple of minutes later, I heard the toilet flush and the faucet sound full blast.

Natalie called, "Do you know when Fynn is coming back?"

"I don't even know where he went," I replied.

"Call Aunt Georgia," Natalie said. "I need a ride."

Her converta-Bug was chugging fine. It was a quarter to six, and Aunt Georgia had to be at the city council meeting by 7:30. "Where to?" I asked.

"The hospital," she replied.

Natalie still hadn't emerged from the bathroom.

Aunt Georgia stood next to me in the hallway. "What happened?" she asked.

I touched the ties of my necklace. "I think it has something to do with the baby," I said, figuring Aunt Georgia would've found out soon enough anyway.

She drummed the bathroom door and called, "I'm right here, little girl. Open up." Bending closer to me, Aunt Georgia whispered, "Where'd your brother take off to?"

"Probably a meeting," I said, trying to keep the fear out of my voice. "Maybe out running."

When Natalie opened the bathroom door, Aunt Georgia wrapped an arm around her and started down the hallway. "Rain," Aunt Georgia said, "you wait here in case Fynn comes home or calls. Tell him I took Natalie to Lawrence Memorial."

"I'm going with you," I answered, following them into the family room. Aunt Georgia is wrong, I thought. They can't just leave me like this.

At the front door, Natalie reached for my hand. "I need Fynn," she said. "Do me a favor. Call the Flash. Tell him the printing company is closed tomorrow for the holiday, so we have to get the paper over there tonight. I'll try to get back to finish the layout, but he might have to handle it by himself. All that's left is plugging in the city council story and dropping everything off at the printer." On the porch steps, she added, "My editorial!"

No matter what she was saying, I knew the deadline wasn't what was scaring her.

"Hush now, little girl," Aunt Georgia said, guiding Natalie. "It'll all get done."

As Aunt Georgia's station wagon pulled out of my driveway, the wind chime rattled, and Chewie began to bark. I stepped back inside, retreated into the kitchen, and gave him a hydrant-shaped dog treat.

My fingers curled through Chewie's soft fur. "Don't worry, boy," I said. "They'll be okay."

When I'd tried calling, nobody answered the newsroom phone, and the machine didn't pick up. The receptionist, Mrs. Grubert, usually goes home at five.

My laptop hummed on the table. When I touched the mouse, the fireworks screen saver was replaced by Natalie's unfinished editorial.

Subject: American Indian Summer Youth Camp
Pros: (1) self-esteem building; (2) team building; (3) educational; (4) need to support diversity; (5) mayor ran on youth programs.
Cons: (1) serves small population; (2) city broke.
Context: $ for (1) city hall renovation; (2) mayor's junket

to Tahiti; (3) Bierfest; (4) July 4 Carnival & BBQ cook-off; (5) swimming pool.

Before shutting off the laptop, I saved the document and prayed, "Dear God, please take care of Natalie. Thank you and amen." I hoped all of the times I'd skipped church wouldn't count against me, and I added, "P.S. What am I supposed to be doing?"

The phone rang. I grabbed the receiver and said, "Go to Lawrence Memorial."

"What happened?" Fynn asked. "I'm in the Jeep, just hit town limits."

It hit me all at once. If he'd been helping Natalie instead of sticking his ostrich head into work, she might not have been on her way to the emergency room. "It's your fiancée," I said, "and the baby you never bothered to tell me about."

Fynn hung up on me, and the dial tone blared.

While waiting for my brother to call back, I counted the thirty-nine roosters line-dancing across the stenciled border of my kitchen and verified that total eleven times. When the kitchen phone rang again, it wasn't Fynn.

"It's a beautiful eighty degrees today here at Andersen Air Force Base," Dad said.

I bit off the hangnail on my pinkie and confided to him what was happening. About Natalie and the baby. That Aunt Georgia wouldn't leave Natalie and Fynn by themselves at the hospital, but without her, the Indian Campers had little chance of outgunning Mrs. Owen at city hall. I kept to myself the part about the pasta bridge and my camera. And

I kept to myself the part about Galen's birthday.

It was only a few hours until the Fourth of July.

"The hardest thing about being overseas," Dad told me, "is that I don't always understand what's going on at home. But I guess you kids would have to fly some solos, even if I were there."

Not wanting him to worry more than necessary, I said, "I'm okay. Really."

"So I gathered," Dad replied. "You're getting out more. Shooting again." When I didn't answer, he added, "Believe me, Rain, I understand. If it hadn't been for you and Fynn, I would've probably headed for the hills when we lost your mom."

"You know," I answered, my hand tighter on the phone, "I thought about that when I stayed home instead of going to Galen's funeral with Grampa and Fynn, and . . ."

Just like that, we started talking about how I'd been since Galen had died. It doesn't really matter, all the things we said. What matters is this: For all the land and ocean between us, Dad had understood more than I ever would've guessed.

As the conversation wound down, he said, "Make sure somebody lets me know what happens with Natalie and the baby ASAP."

Despite everything, I straightened my shoulders and answered, "Yes, sir!"

That's when I realized I wasn't helping anybody by counting stenciled roosters.

Rising Rain

FROM MY JOURNAL:

I was seven and it was summer and my mom was still alive. We cruised south on Highway 169, Okie-bound, windows down, listening to country music, NPR, and static. Just Mom and me in her '68 Mustang coupe.

We pulled over—at maybe it was a Dairy Queen?—for chili dogs with cheese and icy pink lemonades. Then we ran across the busy highway to this antiques store with a Lucky Strike pinball machine and a jukebox playing rock and roll records for a cigar-store Indian. When I crawled back into the shotgun seat of Mom's car, the vinyl seats toasted my rear end through my jeans shorts and seared the backs of my bare thighs.

It was a pretty near perfect day.

JULY 3

The first raindrops struck the concrete walkway behind me as I pushed through the front doors of city hall. The main meeting room was empty except for the flags of Hannesburg, of Kansas, and of the United States. Tarps covered the podium, floors, banisters, and moldings. I smelled sawdust, wood stain, and cigars.

It took me a moment to notice the arrow sign: MEETING, THIS WAY.

The finished basement had been converted into a makeshift conference room. Not that I'd ever bothered to go to a city council meeting before, but without the flags and podium, the setup seemed more like a get-together. Less like a sermon, more like Sunday school. I would've been more worried if Uncle Ed didn't represent Aunt Georgia's district on the city council. The way I figured it, he wouldn't vote against us.

Indian Camp financing was the first item under "New Business." I slipped into the room as Marie finished answering the council's questions, just in time to raise my hand and be counted among the Indian Campers.

Then Uncle Ed excused himself, covering his gold tooth with one hand, saying that voting on a program that would directly benefit his niece would be a conflict of interest.

Last summer, the council had voted to send the mayor to visit Hannesburg's sister city on the tropical island of Tahiti. That's why he ran for reelection on youth development, instead of on fiscal responsibility. That's what inspired Mrs. Owen's campaign committee to dub him "Tahiti, the Piña Colada Politician." He did go with the nickname and began always wearing tropical shirts and shades.

And at the meeting Mayor Rummel did support our financing request for Indian Camp, at least in the discussion before the vote. But the vote itself was two to one against.

Because I'd joined Indian Camp, Uncle Ed had stepped

down. Because Uncle Ed had stepped down, he hadn't been able to tie the vote. Because Uncle Ed hadn't tied the vote, the mayor didn't have to vote at all. (In Hannesburg, mayors only cast tiebreakers.) Because the mayor didn't vote, he couldn't look bad for voting one way or the other.

If Mrs. Owen had been trying to save the city money, she'd won. If she'd just been trying to make the mayor look bad, it had all been for nothing.

As for me, I'd joined Indian Camp to support Aunt Georgia and my friends. But, figuring the mayor would've voted yes if he'd had the chance, there was at least a possibility that my hand going up had blown the whole deal.

Then Queenie turned in her chair and smiled at me the way she used to when we were second-best friends. She must have appreciated my showing up. She probably thought it was my way of apologizing for the broken bridge and maybe even for our most recent battle. That would be just like Queenie, embracing the feeling of the moment.

I waved back.

From behind the head table, Mayor Tahiti Rummel pushed up his sunglasses, pounded his gavel, and called a five-minute recess, probably figuring nobody in the audience wanted to sit through round thirteen of the Great Swimming Pool Debate. The topic of the day was location: whether the downtown site should be revamped or whether another hole should be dug in the new subdivision.

I rushed past the three rows of fold-out chairs—past the Indian Campers, Mrs. Headbird, Mrs. Burnham, and the Washingtons—to the Flash, whose front-row seat was five chairs to the right of Mrs. Owen.

Chin high, she passed us on her way out, and I let her go, wondering if she'd ever manage to boot Tahiti out of office and whether that would make her feel better.

Meanwhile, the Indian Campers and their supporters gathered in a circle toward the back of the room, and I saw Mr. Washington shaking Tahiti's hand. Dmitri glanced my way, and I could feel the invitation. But right then, I had more to worry about than patching myself into that crowd.

"Natalie's not feeling so hot," I informed the Flash. "Can you finish the layout, your city council story, write something for the editorial page, and drop it off at the printer?" It sounded like a lot of work. I hoped he could handle it. From what Natalie had told me, the Flash had completed only one semester of college reporting and a two-year stint on his St. Louis high-school paper.

"No problem, Shooter," he said, patting his coat pocket. "It's for times like this that I carry tequila."

ꕥ MAMAS AND BABES

FROM MY JOURNAL:

It was an old fight, the kind that shakes a home and all the souls inside. Mama asked Daddy to retire from the service. He claimed he couldn't get any other kind of job.

"Our life is here," she argued. "I don't want my kids growing up overseas."

"Their home, your home, is with me," he said. "Not Kansas, or Oklahoma."

She didn't answer. Instead, Mama came into my room to tuck me in beneath my broken-star quilt. She kissed my forehead, turned off the lamp on my wicker nightstand, and whispered, "Don't fret, Rainy Day. Sometimes grown-ups have to bicker. It clears out all the bad stuff that builds up inside us over the years."

Mama died the next day.

When the base finally closed, Dad wouldn't consider taking Fynn and me to South Korea, and there's been no talk about the two of us moving to Guam.

JULY 3

When I got home, the red light on the phone was blinking.

The message was from Fynn. "Rain? Are you

there? We're at the hospital. I'll call when I know something."

A second message. Fynn again. "Rain, please pick up. Okay, okay, we're still at the hospital. I shouldn't have hung up on you today. Don't freak out."

A third. "Rain? Rain, where are you? I'm sorry. I didn't mean to leave you hanging like that. Natalie's okay, and she didn't lose the baby. We're just going to take extra-good care of them and pray for the best. Okay, baby sister?"

After we'd finally gotten Natalie settled in the master bedroom, she said, "You can tell people, Rain, about the baby. Run it on page one. Rent a billboard. Put it on CNN. I can't believe I'd been worried about what anyone might say."

I took a breath and launched into my confession. "I know this probably isn't the best time to tell you," I said, "but I sort of joined Indian Camp."

"You're fired," she replied, pulling the kite's tail quilt under her chin.

I'd expected as much.

Fynn grinned, apparently unconcerned with the destruction of my fledgling career.

"Just for this story," Natalie added. "I saw some of your work in the darkroom at the *Examiner*. It's more textured somehow, more storytelling. Besides, we need the art." She reached for my hand. "Rain, could you check on the Flash for me? I think I'd rest better with an eyewitness report."

ꕥ DEADLINES

FROM MY JOURNAL:

Seventh grade. Five-thirty A.M. *Someone knocked on my bedroom window.*

When I got up to check, Queenie was standing on the other side.

"What do you know?" she asked, all dimples and sunshine.

"It's Saturday," I replied. "I'm not a morning person. Ever heard of a doorbell?"

Queenie explained that she hadn't wanted to wake up the whole house, and then she asked me to come with her. "Please," she said. "It's my parents' fifteenth anniversary."

I didn't budge. "Try Galen."

"I don't want Galen." Queenie folded her arms. "You're my best friend."

I never knew what to expect when she said that. But it meant trouble or magic.

I got dressed and left a note on the kitchen table.

Queenie and I spent all morning making phone calls, going from business to business and house to house. At noon, Grampa drove us to Lawrence for supplies.

By six o'clock, the cars and trucks parked on the street had been rearranged. Only one spot remained open—the one at the end of the block. By 6:30, everyone in town had gathered, hiding inside the stores. By 6:45, we had the ammunition passed out. At 6:55, the Washingtons parked their Oldsmobile in the only empty spot.

As they climbed out of the car, people streamed out of the doors and lined up along the sidewalk.

Our coconspirators blew soap bubbles from wands as the couple passed by on their way to Oma Dottie's B&B. The bubbles rose, thousands, luminous.

"I feel like a bride all over again," Mrs. Washington declared.

That had been a gift. I'd been proud to be part of it. I loved Queenie back then.

"I'm running your pictures," the Flash announced as I walked into the newsroom.

"But—"

"You're off the payroll," he said, eyes back on the computer monitor. "I know. Fynn just called. But the pages are way too gray without the art, and the bottom line is that Natalie left me in charge."

I glanced at the pages being pasted up on the light table. The art, photos, and copy were all in place, but there was a gaping hole on the editorial page. I knew that's where Natalie's op-ed piece on Indian Camp was supposed to run. I took a few steps to the second table and saw that the Flash's city council story wasn't in place yet, either. From the scowl on his face, I guessed both articles were still in progress.

Except for the Flash and me, the newsroom was empty. Mrs. Grubert had closed the reception desk hours earlier. Mrs. Burnham had already finished laying out the ads and left for the day. The Flash's flask of tequila sat on his desk.

"Don't miss me too much," I said. "Natalie says she'll be hiring me back on for future stories."

"Miss you nothing, Shooter," the Flash replied, shifting in his trench coat. "I'm counting on you to help me out. The city council piece is done, so I'm working on my Indian Camp project until I can come up with something to write for the editorial page."

He explained that since he was covering Indian Camp as a news piece, it wasn't considered ethical for him to write an editorial about it. And because the Indian Camp project would be laid out on four full pages, he'd be working steadily on it until next week, when the whole thing would finally run.

"You're fair game for a source now," the Flash added, "and I've got a key question for you."

That wasn't why I'd jogged over to the newsroom, but I figured, Why not? If I could help him, then my report to Natalie would be a bit more positive. Anything for the cause. I pulled a chair up to face the Flash across his desk, noticing that Oreo wrappers littered the industrial-tile floor. I smiled, trying to reassure him.

The Flash picked up his pen and looked squarely at me, all business. "Okay," he began. "Now, I asked Mrs. Wilhelm about the pasta bridge." When I winced at the memory of its destruction, he added, "Sorry, but she said something about 'fostering teamwork'"—he squinted at the scribbled notes on his pad of paper—"and being a retired science teacher . . . and it being something she could teach from her own expertise. That's all great—and forgive me if I'm just dense, but why a pasta bridge?"

I swiped a rubber band from his desk and twirled it around my index finger. "If they'd tried to build a real bridge, Spence would've probably killed himself. His parents would've sued. It would've been a real tragedy. Front page." I frowned. "We missed an opportunity. Could've been the highlight of your string book."

The Flash smirked. "Thanks, Shooter. Big help there. Fine, take pity on me. What does building a bridge have to do with the Native American youth program?"

The rubber band went flying. He was serious.

Being a mixed-blood girl is no big deal. Really. It seems weird to have to say this, but after a lifetime of experience, I'm used to being me. Dealing with the rest of the world and its ideas, now that makes me a little crazy sometimes. But the Flash seemed like a pretty open-minded guy. And, sure, I would've been tempted to make fun of him anyway, but he was trying hard.

I thought for a moment. What was I supposed to say? It was just so obvious. "Do you have any idea," I began, "how weird it is to be an Indian in Hannesburg, Kansas?"

The Flash didn't look impressed. "Do you have any idea," he answered, "how weird it is to be Jewish in Hannesburg, Kansas?"

"You're Jewish?" I asked.

"My whole life." He leaned back, threading his fingers behind his head.

The thought shot through my head like a bottle

rocket. "But you don't seem . . ." Oops, I thought, sinking slightly in the chair. I wished again for that word-catcher to let the good words through and trap the rest. Maybe I should be the person to invent it.

"I don't seem *what*?" the Flash asked, shifting forward, elbows on the desktop.

"You don't seem to talk about it much." Good save, I thought.

He grinned. "You don't seem to talk about being a Native American much, either."

Personally, for the past couple of weeks, I'd felt like nobody had been talking about anything else. It was beginning to get on my nerves.

When I didn't respond, the Flash added, "So enlighten me. What does bridge building have to do with Native American culture?"

At that point, I didn't have much choice. I just laid it out. "Indians build bridges."

He scribbled down my answer and looked back at me. "This is some kind of metaphor, right? You trying to Yoda me or something, Sci-fi Girl? Fine, I'll play: Why do Indians build bridges?"

At least he hadn't asked about why we were building the Indian Camp website.

I shrugged. "To cross rivers."

"Rivers," the Flash repeated. "Like rivers of wisdom?"

"Highways," I added, slightly annoyed but honestly trying to help.

"Highways?" he echoed.

I took a breath and folded my hands in my lap. "The

summer Fynn was seventeen, he built a wooden bridge over a two-foot-high concrete troll at the miniature golf course behind Phillips 66 Car Wash."

No reaction.

"You can check it out for yourself," I added. "The paint is chipped off of the troll's nose, and its eyes look possessed. Nice bridge, though."

The Flash's eyes were blank. He still wasn't getting it.

Against my better judgment, I tried one more time. "Think of it like this: How is bridge building not an Indian thing?"

"Well, Indians . . . You just don't think . . ." The Flash rubbed his eyelids. "Well, maybe *you* do. I just always thought of Native American culture being . . ."

It wasn't like I was in a position to blame him. After all, nobody says the wrong thing more often than me. But I couldn't resist teasing just a little bit. In my best Hollywood Indian voice, I said, "Bridges not for white man only."

"Nice," the Flash answered. He opened his flask of tequila and took a swig. "Well, good. Got it. And, hey, I don't feel stupid or anything. So Indians build bridges."

I replied, "Not all of us. Not me. At least not when I'm packing a camera."

The Flash didn't seem to appreciate my joke. The look he gave me was half-defensive, half-innocent. He set the flask back on the cluttered desktop. "You know, I never even met a Native American before this summer."

Poor guy. It was time to fess up. "If it makes you feel any better," I began, "all I know about Jewish people, I learned from *Fiddler on the Roof.*"

For a moment, we were both quiet. Then the Flash tossed down his pen and started laughing. Before long, I joined in. It wasn't funny, how clueless both of us were. But laughing worked better than medicine.

After we calmed down, the Flash asked, "You're feeling better, Shooter?"

It was a serious question and took me off guard. But of course he'd probably heard my best friend had died not long ago and my mother a few years before. That was part of my story, and he was in the business of asking questions. It came naturally to him. And by now, I was sure Natalie had briefed the Flash before teaming us up, if only out of fairness. After all, if my dog had died, too, my life story would probably qualify for the lyrics of a country-music song.

I stood to leave, suddenly determined. "Yeah," I said. "I'm feeling all right."

After I got home and gave my eyewitness report on the Flash to Natalie, Fynn followed me to his Domain and agreed to let me use his newest computer, the one with more bells than Santa's sleigh and more whistles than a stadium full of referees. A biography about Billy Mills lay open on the laser printer.

Fynn set a plate of two strawberry jelly sandwiches between us on the makeshift desk, a three-by-six wood plank propped on four pillars of stacked cement blocks. He reached into the minifridge, pulled out a can of Cherry Coke for me and a bottle of Coors for himself, and then sat his backside on a wooden crate.

"Sorry about the city council meeting," Fynn said. "I didn't like Mrs. Owen referring to you in her letter to the editor. Or to Galen. She was bad enough before he died, but since then, she's run over half the people in town with her Mourning Mother Meets Grim Reaper act." Fynn popped the cap off his beer, took a long drink, and added, "I admire what Aunt Georgia is doing, but, you know, the city can't afford to allocate that much for programs like Indian Camp. From what Uncle Ed has told me, Tahiti is practically spending this town into bankruptcy. Mrs. Owen is right about that."

I started in on my sandwich, in no mood to debate politics with my big brother, Mr. Fiscal Responsibility himself. After all the nagging he'd done to try to get me to sign up, neither Natalie nor I could understand why Fynn wasn't completely supporting Indian Camp. She'd even asked me about it, and all I could think to say was that he took after Dad.

"You've been talking to Natalie," he guessed. "Hey, don't look at me like that. I love her, too, you know." He took another swig, then said, "But if the girl buys a rocking chair at a garage sale instead of quick-drawing her gold card at Dillard's, it's breaking news."

I clicked to a search engine, and the cursor blinked at me. I had no idea what to type in. Fynn turned on a Meat Loaf CD, keeping the volume low.

"On a deadline?" I asked, listening to "All Revved Up with No Place to Go."

"No," he answered. "I think you are. Galen's birthday, right?"

"How'd you know?" I asked, surprised.

Fynn shook his head slowly. "I am your big brother, remember? And even if he was your best friend, not mine, it's easy to remember birthdays that fall on holidays."

Fynn's beer was already half-gone, and he hadn't touched his sandwich. His prized Jerry Garcia tie looked wilted, worn-out. I wondered if his impending fatherhood and matrimony had been the inspirations for his corporate makeover. I would've bet on it.

"You're going to be a great dad," I said, glancing at the Billy Mills book and typing "Olympics." "Remember how you taught Galen and me to do Java programming?"

"Yeah," Fynn answered, sounding surprised. He'd caught me saying Galen's name out loud, but we didn't have to talk about it. Fynn's voice grew quieter as he added, "Of course I do."

I twisted the cap off of my Cherry Coke, toasted him, and did my own preacher imitation: "Your patience will bring you joy and glory, Brother Fynnegan. Why, Miss Natalie is a lucky woman to have landed herself such a fine and righteous young man. That, I say, now *that* you must believe."

Fynn looked past me somehow, apparently not amused. "About my engagement," he finally said. "Mine and *Natalie's* engagement. . . . We're pushing back the wedding date indefinitely. If anyone asks, we've decided to wait and save up for a bigger wedding, something to make the Lewises proud. It's partly true anyway."

That didn't sound good. I fixed my eyes on the Web page in front of me, titled "World's Greatest Athletes," and took a sip of my Cherry Coke. "You just said you love her," I reminded him.

"I do" was Fynn's answer.

"Well, are you going to marry her or not?" I shot back.

"I hope so," he said. "We'll see."

Independence Day

FROM MY JOURNAL:

It was the same trip, the one when I was seven, riding in the front seat next to my mom in her Mustang on the way to Oklahoma. We went with my grandparents, Aunt Louise, and Cousin Margo to picnics and powwows, to social and stomp dances.

I can still smell the pork cooking, taste the lukewarm coleslaw, hear the songs, and feel the rhythm of the shell-shakers. I remember ribbons and tear dresses and me trying to dance like Mama. Echoes of stories, the snapping of fire. Smoke rising to heaven, and how it stung my eyes. Talk of the corn and of the New Year.

Fynn and I go to First Baptist because it's the church Dad grew up in. But there are plenty of Baptist Creeks in Oklahoma.

Back when I was seven, I didn't have to think about what I believed and where I belonged. I just did.

JULY 4

I awoke in Fynn's chair in his Domain, wrapped in the broken-star quilt Mom had started the day she found out she was pregnant with me. My big brother must have returned sometime during the night and done his best to tuck me in.

Walking outside with the quilt still wrapped around my shoulders, I noticed the sun had brought long shadows. A tiny spider scrambled over my bare foot, and we both went on our way.

A couple of steps later, I inspected a series of fresh chalk drawings that decorated the full length of my front walk—from Donau Lane to my porch steps.

First, a boy using a long wooden pole to push his canoe through a river crowded with tall stalks, more realistic because of the weeds growing through the cracked concrete.

A four-foot-long rendition of the pasta bridge, complete with the Chinese umbrella.

And finally, a girl with wheat brown hair, her face hidden behind a camera.

The artist had created his mural while I'd slept. Dmitri, I realized. It had to be. For a moment, it felt like my birthday.

Inside the house, I made a phone call to Spence, ducked into my bedroom, and opened my hope chest. Inspired in part by Dmitri, I fetched my photo collection and returned to Fynn's Domain. It was finally time to face Galen.

The first photo: our third-grade lemonade stand, shot by Grampa. Galen and I standing in my front yard behind a card table, chins up, hands clasped behind backs. The sign read 25 CENTS OR A BASEBALL CARD.

The second: Galen chowing down on some of the

results of our fifth-grade science project: Which Brand of Popcorn Is the Poppingest? Photo by yours truly. We'd only scored a white participation ribbon at the school fair, but we celebrated by threading our test materials into a garland and stringing it on my Christmas tree.

The third: Galen last summer, sitting on his front step, holding the wand of a dangling cat toy. Angel leapt for the cluster of feathers flying at the end of its bouncing cord. "Cat fishing," Galen had called it. Once again, photo by me.

I scanned in my favorites—a picture of Galen and me sitting with our arms around each other in the bleachers at the powwow (photo by Mrs. Georgia Wilhelm) and one I'd taken of him inhaling turquoise cotton candy on our second-grade adventure at the American Royal Rodeo. To the right of the picture, I keyed in:

Galen Hannes Owen
Best Friend, World's Greatest Athlete, Partner in Crime
"Weeping may endure for a night,
but joy cometh in the morning."
—Psalms 30:5

I remembered Galen, spinning in the snowy soccer field with his arms outstretched, protesting the make-believe scores he'd earned at an imaginary swing-jump contest. Leave it to the journalists to write up the everyday facts in obituaries.

This was my truth about Galen.

* * *

When Spence finally showed up at Fynn's Domain, I asked, "Did you get it?"

Spence had both of his hands behind his back. "Queenie will let you use it on one condition," he said.

I swiveled from the computer screen and folded my arms, waiting.

"You help us rebuild our pasta bridge," he bargained, "and you can use the poem."

A generous offer. "Deal," I answered, pleased with it.

"We're going for fifteen pounds," Spence warned me.

Ambitious. Maybe I would even look through my prints for a picture to scan on the Indian Camp Web page, if Dmitri didn't already have drawings ready to go.

Spence tossed me a folded-up piece of notebook paper, held up a bag from McDonald's, and announced, "Lunch."

As Spence and I finished our fries, I tilted my head to the screen and asked, "What do you think?" I'd set up the pictures diagonally, flush left on top and flush right on the bottom, with the tombstonelike copy next to the powwow photo. I'd left a space next to the rodeo photo for Queenie's poem. The background was turquoise, like cotton candy.

"I don't know," Spence said, sitting on the crate. "It depends. Are you girls ever going to stop fighting over this dead white guy and give me a shot?"

It took me thirty seconds to realize he'd actually said that out loud and another thirty to realize I could actually stop myself from telling him off. It had been jealousy talking and maybe just a splash of something more fierce, like between Queenie and me, like between Natalie and Lorelei.

A second later, I realized Spence might be as interested in me as in anyone else. Maybe more interested. It was time for me to start focusing on what was happening now and what might happen in the future. But Spence seemed too smooth, and I'd caught him sneaking looks at girls besides me.

"Marie turned you down?" I asked him.

"Flat," he answered.

"Queenie?" I inquired.

"Same," Spence replied.

I settled back in Fynn's chair and fired one more question: "That right?"

"Right as Rain."

I preferred the Pez jokes.

Before I could even begin to untangle my feelings, Spence asked, "You know what's weird about you?"

I wasn't sure I wanted to know.

"Your eyes are brown today," he said, "and it's starting to cloud over. They were gray yesterday, during the storm. Green when it's sunny, like that day in the park. They change colors with the weather."

"Hazel," I said, just a reflex, and then stopped a minute. No jokes. No teasing. No one had noticed since Mom. Heat rushed to my cheeks, and I suddenly felt embarrassed. Truth was, besides Galen, I didn't have any real experience with boys.

The HHS junior varsity cheerleaders picked that

moment to cruise my dead-end street, hooting for Fynn. News of his engagement apparently hadn't reached them. Grateful for the chance to make a joke, I asked Spence, "Why don't you try your luck with them?"

"All right," he said, going to the door, "but I'll see you at Indian Camp, and after that, there's always the Internet."

After Spence left, I ran a fingertip along the seed beads on my necklace and opened the folded piece of notebook paper. In proud, curly letters, Queenie's poem read:

People Talk

We say a lot
to hear ourselves speak
to make ourselves known
to reach out to somebody else.
But what would we say
if only we knew
that our next words
would be our last?
I had a chance to speak,
and speak I did
about secrets and dancing and choices.
But I never took the chance
to speak to you
about life and friendship and love.

Highly cheesy, in my opinion—not that I was in a position to talk. But the poem was classic Queenie—showy, smart-sounding, full of feelings and attitude. Nothing new. So why was it affecting me so much? Why did it feel like my throat was closing up?

No contest. In all the world, for all of his life, Queenie,

Mrs. Owen, and I were the three people who'd most loved Galen.

When he'd died, Queenie stepped right up. She wrote her poem, and she read it out loud in her clear soprano voice to our fellow HMS eighth graders, the coffee-shop gossips, and the distant cousins who'd come to tell Galen good-bye. Then she let go of her grief enough to move on to her next phase. I don't know what it was. Ice sculpture? Herbal healing? Maybe mining for gold. Later, she'd heard from her aunt Suzanne about their Native heritage and joined Indian Camp. Queenie had even found a new friend in Marie.

Not Mrs. Owen. She'd written letters to the editor, collected petition signatures, and run against Tahiti for mayor. But in all those months, Mrs. Owen hadn't asked the moms and cops what kids did come summertime when there was no local pool. She hadn't taken the time to shake any hands, to pass out surveys, to understand the truck drivers, grocery store clerks, and website designers she hoped to represent. She hadn't connected with anything but busyness.

Me? I'd cleaned the house, read sci-fi fan fiction, and eavesdropped in Internet chat rooms. But in all those months, I hadn't taken the time to find out how Natalie felt about her mother, to realize Fynn fretted over an unplanned baby, or to run the cracked sidewalks with Chewie. When I'd finally picked up my camera again, I'd used it as a wall instead of as a window.

Since Galen had died, Mrs. Owen and I had been spinning in place. It was a luminous place because his light still glowed within it, but a chilly place because he really wasn't there. Now I was finally finding my footing again. The dizziness, the nausea, the grief, the guilt, and the self-pity were finally letting go of me.

After I'd coded Queenie's poem and uploaded Galen's memorial onto the server, I logged on to my personal account, which cheerfully informed me that I had mail. A message from Grampa—a man who'd thought the Internet was the latest advancement in fish-retrieval technology, at least until I'd shown him how to send e-mail, just before he'd left for his trip. The message read:

Dear Rainbow,

I've found my pot of gold. That's right, me and Clementine got hitched last night by a fella dressed up as the King (can't wait to show Georgia the pictures). I know the relations will spit sparks about me rushing into this. But I'm getting to be an old man, and it's high time I did some living. Just wanted you to be the first to know. We'll tell those other shirttail relations when we're good and ready.

Viva Las Vegas!

XOXO, Grampa

P.S. Clementine and me are holed up at someplace called an Internet café. Never knew there were so many flavors of coffee.

⚘ Children of the Corn

FROM MY JOURNAL:

The foulmouthed high-school boys were twice as fast as Galen and I because they were cheating by skipping every few stalks. So I was hurrying even more than usual.

What with the rows planted so close together, I got turned around, and Galen was too far ahead to hear my shouts for help. The field spanned enormously. Grasshoppers leapt at my eyes, and I ran like something angry with fangs was chasing me. One leaf ripped skin from the tip of my nose. Another cut a bloody line across the bridge of it.

When I reached the edge of the field, ready to strangle Galen for talking me into taking the job, he choked out, "But you're an Indian, and Indians . . . like corn."

I grabbed his sweaty flannel shirt, pulled his sunburned nose to my bleeding one, and only semicalmly explained in detail exactly how I felt.

JULY 4

Sometimes, I need a box of Cracker Jacks. Need it like air or water or a good night's sleep. I closed out all of my programs, realizing Hein's Grocery Barn would probably lock up early for the holiday, and left Fynn's Domain.

On the way to the store, Chewie and I peeked in on the Fourth of July Carnival and Barbecue Cook-Off. Like every Independence Day and Bierfest weekend, red-and-white-striped tents dotted the park and an assortment of booths lined the sidewalk along Lincoln Avenue. Old men gossiped on the benches. Mommies tied floating balloons to baby strollers. The gazebo had become a makeshift stage for a barbershop quartet.

During setup that morning, Mrs. Owen—reportedly exclaiming "Who needs all this room?"—had donated one side of the merchants' association tent to Dmitri and Marie. Who knows why Mrs. Owen did it. For votes maybe or to soothe a guilty conscience. Or maybe it was an act of kindness. After all, she is Galen's mom. I want to think the best of her. But, sure, I'll continue to keep my distance.

Dmitri and Marie were selling two-dollar cups of wild-rice soup to raise money for the Great Lakes trip. By the time I arrived that afternoon, the Headbirds had made eighty-eight bucks. I was quick to add my two-dollar contribution.

"Plan B," Marie said, handing me a cup of soup.

At that point, we still were $1,250 short. I seriously doubted Aunt Georgia would stick the whole thing on her credit card, and that's a lot of cash.

Although Dmitri had made a point of petting Chewie, he hadn't said much to me. I wanted to thank him for the chalk mural, but I didn't want to embarrass him in front of Marie. That conversation would have to wait.

My first spoonful of light brown rice was nutty, tender,

mixed with chicken and broth. Each grain had opened and rounded like a tiny butterfly. As I polished off my soup, I began believing that we might actually make it to the reservation and that it might not be too late for me to connect with the Ojibway side of my heritage. Even if my family had come from Saginaw, not Leech Lake, it would be a start.

I was finally about to mention it to Dmitri and Marie, when Spence jogged to the tent and asked, "Everybody recovered from local politics?"

"The council was fairly respectful," Marie said. "It's not like they sat there and made fun of us. Maybe I should've said something different, better, to convince them. I was so nervous."

Spence popped his gum. "Nah, they were the lame ones," he said, "not you."

"Never would've made it without your suggestion," Marie answered. She went on to explain, "Spence told me to pretend they were Pez heads."

Chewie barked, like he was laughing, and then I felt myself smile.

High above, Queenie and Ernie rounded the top of the Ferris wheel. I thought back to the day we'd made her mom feel like a bride and wondered if we might someday become friends again. Maybe I could sit by her at church next Sunday.

A few minutes later, I stood in front of Lorelei at the checkout counter.

"How's your brother?" she asked, ringing up my purchase.

"Wonderful," I answered. "Ready for fatherhood."

"Oh," Lorelei replied, tapping register buttons, "they're planning to have kids."

"They're already pregnant," I said, taking advantage of Natalie's green light. If people were going to talk, they could hear it from us first. I handed Lorelei a five-dollar bill and added, "Cool, don't you think?"

"Sure," Lorelei said, tossing my bill into her cash drawer. "You must be thrilled." She recovered and gave me my change. "Are you celebrating at the fireworks festival?" she asked. "Maybe with a certain retired teacher's visiting nephew? Or that new boy from the trailer park?"

I grabbed my three-pack of Cracker Jacks and answered, "I've got plans with another male. A wild one. We're going to run like night creatures and howl at the moon."

What Really Happened

JULY 4
FROM MY JOURNAL:

Today, the black wrought-iron gate didn't stop me. I hiked up a manicured hill at the Garden of Roses Cemetery to a simple grave marker set beneath a maple tree. The stone was flat and gray like Galen's, but it wasn't him I'd come to see. I thought about Mama, cradled by the earth, about how wonderful and safe that must be.

On her stone, I placed four peach roses—one each for Dad, Fynn, Natalie, and me. I told Mama about baby Aiyana. I promised to tell the baby stories, so that from them, she'd know the gramma who'd gone by the same name.

Finally, I left without stopping by Galen's grave. The wound from losing Mama was deeper, but the one from losing Galen was still too fresh.

Next time, maybe.

Chewie and I watched the fireworks explode over Burnham's Apple Orchard. They all glittered a moment, lingering, and then faded, one after the other, like the smoky trails of fallen snakes. I was flying, just barely, back and forth on the same swing as last New Year's

Eve. Galen's ghost soared nearby.

Aunt Georgia called this morning and mentioned that Queenie's great-grandfather had been a Seminole, which made Queenie a pretty close cousin after all. I was more interested in the fact that Queenie had volunteered to make Thursday's spaghetti dinner. Definitely an Italian cooking phase. We planned to meet at my house, and everybody had been invited—families and friends.

The Flash called, too. Lacking any better ideas last night, he drank too much tequila and wrote an editorial called "Life in the Heartland." Should be a scream.

Now that I thought about it, it was hard to imagine Queenie dumping Galen for Ernie and being afraid to tell me so. She was much more up front than I'd ever been.

I decided that she was telling the truth—that Galen broke up with her on the day of the dance.

He had asked me about whether I'd date a black person. A secret part of my heart had wondered, even then, if he'd backed away from Queenie because of her race. And I'd never dared to ask him about it, but there was a time when I wondered if my being Native was the reason he'd never made a first move on me.

The rest of my heart knew better. Galen had backed out because of his mother. He hadn't been happy about caving in, being the mama's boy, or losing Queenie. Even though he'd never spelled out exactly what had happened, I'd taken that to mean he wasn't the one who'd made the decision. I'd been too jealous to see what was really going on. It had all started with the "no dating" rule meant to protect him. Mrs. Owen had won that round. At least as close as she'd come to winning.

Maybe Galen had underestimated how I'd react. Maybe he hadn't realized I'd toss Queenie out of my locker and out of my life. Maybe once I'd lashed out at her, Galen had been afraid to tell me the whole truth. What I knew for sure was that, at some point, he'd led me on about what had happened between them. He'd let me think the worst of Queenie. I blamed him for that. But I let it burn through, and I let it go. Blame wasn't something I cared to hold on to.

The memories wouldn't let go.

All I could think about was what happened between Galen and me that last night, last New Year's Eve. No, I didn't take my sweater off, and Galen didn't take my sweater off. I wasn't even wearing a sweater. I was wearing my black silk shirt, the one Aunt Louise had shipped me for Christmas. The one that made me feel sexy and sophisticated.

Besides, what if I had peeled it? With my bottle-cap boobs, what could I have done next? Handed Galen a magnifying glass?

FROM MY JOURNAL:

This is what really happened that night.

Dragging my high-tops to slow myself, I fiddled with my camera strap. My lips itched, and my heart did a two-step. I rose from my swing. It was happy birthday time.

I walked to Galen in the confetti snow, and he stopped midspin, swinging his arms, off balance. I wanted to count his tasty-looking freckles and tease my fingers through his nose-long bangs. But I couldn't risk my courage, and I couldn't waste another chilled breath.

He closed his sweeping golden eyelashes, and I closed my stubby dark ones.

It was only one kiss. It wasn't a deep kiss, a French kiss, the kind of kiss that redefines a teen life. It was pepperoni, snowflakes, spit, and rodeo dust. Crazy, like dancing and soaring and walking to a new home.

Sweeter because it didn't taste like good-bye.

Author's Note

If you look on a map, you will not find Hannesburg, Kansas. If you look in the Douglas County phone book, its people and businesses are unlisted—along with a few other places and publications mentioned in this book.

However, Douglas County does exist, along with Haskell Indian Nations University, the University of Kansas, Shawnee Mission West High School, and both Lawrence and Overland Park.

But this story is a work of fiction. Its characters stand on their own, separate from the real-life Indian community and Native American youth programs in Kansas.

While this novel was in progress, my much-loved grandfather, Clifford Pokagon Smith, died of cancer. He'll always be missed. For those of you facing a loss in your own lives, I hope that this story offered some comfort.